D0578069

dry RAIN

dry RAIN

STORIES BY

PETE FROMM

Lyons & Burford, Publishers

Printed in the United States of America

1 3 5 7 9 10 8 6 4 2

Library of Congress Cataloging-in-Publication Data

Fromm, Pete, 1958–
Dry rain ; stories / by Pete Fromm.
p.   cm.
ISBN 1-55821-554-9 (cloth)
I. Title
PS3556.R5942D78   1997
813'.54—DC21   97-4000
CIP

I am grateful to the following publications in which these stories originally appeared: Glimmer Train: "Dry Rain," "Helmets," and "The Topic of Cancer" (as "Six Inches of Water"). Puerto del Sol: "Dutch Elm." Vignette: "Lifesaving." American Way: "Play Ball" and "Headwaters" (as "Solitude"). Cream City Review: "The Baby-Sitter." Kinesis: "Sage and Salt." Talking River Review: "Slipping." Big Sky Journal: "Chinook." Manoa: "Feller." "Helmets" also appeared in the anthology Family: A Celebration, and "Dutch Elm" in The Writers Community Twentieth Anniversary Anthology.

I'd also like to again thank Ruth McLaughlin and John Daniel for their help with early drafts of many of these stories, and David Duncan and William Marcus for helping nudge the book into its final form.

Closest to my heart, the stories can only be for Rose

c o n t e n t s

h o o t

The elk keep devouring my haystacks so I'm only in town for bullets—a quick trip to the hardware—no plans to stop and talk to anybody. But waiting at the checkout I get that hinky feeling somebody's watching me. I glance down the aisle, but there's nobody there. Making like I'm just looking over the power tools, I take a peek behind me. Only one there is a Hutterite woman, who looks straight at the floor as soon as I see her.

Turning back to the counter, I wipe a little sweat from underneath my jacket collar. Me sweating it over a Hoot, I think, shaking my head. Like she'd be the one staring.

I watch the lady scratching away at my receipt until slowly I realize what I'd seen behind me. At first glance it was just another Hutterite, waiting for the men haggling over steel prices—same long homemade dress, same polka-dot scarf. But somehow she seems different, thinner maybe, or younger. I feel her watching me again.

So I turn around, stare right at her this time. I mean, they must be used to that, right? First thing I see is she doesn't have the standard Hutterite glasses, thick as trough ice. Her eyes are the same watery blue though, and she drops them again as soon as she sees mine. So I take an extra look.

You hardly ever see young ones. Especially girls, unless they're real little. And you never see pretty ones. This one's taller than most, the bright colors of her dress drawn in tighter and stretched out longer than I can ever remember seeing, though, of course, I've never spent much time studying Hoots. But I'm still studying this one when she looks back up, right at me, her eyes never wavering, like she can see thoughts.

For a second I don't turn away but then she smiles and I feel caught. I'm sweating all over and I can't even smile back. I turn to the lady at the register and scooping up my bullets, I say, "Just skip the receipt," and jump the few steps back out to the cold and wind. There are more Hutterites out there, gabbling along in German or whatever, going quiet as I pass.

I fire up my truck, but then wait a minute, watching the Hoots by the door; the old women thick as tree trunks, the men in their black homemades, with their black beards and no mustaches. I wonder how the girl could have come from anything like them—what it must be like having a smile like hers, stuck out in a colony with all of them. With the wind tugging at the tails of their coats they look like ravens, and when they glance my way I take off.

By the time I get home the blow off the mountains is moaning through the windbreaks so instead of working on the last stretch of fence I go inside. I wind up walking from room to empty room, turning lights on and then off, listening to the windows rattle in their frames, wishing there was somebody I could tell about the Hutterite girl.

The stairs echo under my boots, reminding me of Carlton thumping up them after Mom whaled on him for one of his outrages. I think maybe I'll write Carlton a letter about the girl, but he's clear down in Texas, working offshore oil. I feel like calling, but Carlton once told me there aren't any phones on the rigs. Not that

I could afford a call like that anyway, for nothing but a Hoot girl smiling at me in town.

I find a pad of paper and an old envelope and set them on the kitchen table but by then it's finally dark enough to go out to the hay.

The sky's pretty clear and I walk to the stacked bales without using the light. I crawl up to wait for the elk. They've been at it every night lately and my plan is to pop one, hoping it'll scare the rest off. I'm no hunter, but I figure it's what Carlton would do. He was always shooting something.

Mom, of course, always treated the elk like pets and wouldn't let Carlton near them. But, back up on the hill with Dad, I doubt Mom knows a thing about what goes on down here. I kept the graves like a golf green all summer, but now wish I'd let them grow. The elk would probably graze there if I had, and if Mom could know anything now, I bet she'd like that.

The elk are slow tonight and the moon starts wisping in and out of the clouds, the light going from silvery to a kind of foggy black-gray, mostly light enough to see. The wind's still whipping though, and lying freezing in the darkness I get to thinking of later, of crawling between the crackling cold sheets alone. I think of the Hoot girl's eyes, the blue so watered down they were spooky, like glass. When I was a kid we tortured ourselves with the rumor that the Hutterites got so inbred in their colonies they'd pay men to sleep with their wives. Tall, blond, blue-eyed men. Like me. The older guys, like Carlton, said it wasn't much, like they did it all the time. Carlton said there was always a sheet between you, with just a strategic hole, and that the girl just lay there. I'm glad I didn't write him any letter.

Not that I believe any of that about doing it through the sheets. They say all kinds of things about the Hutterites; like they only sell their worn-out roosters at the farmer's market, or things are so expensive downtown because they shoplift so much.

I don't know. The only Hutterites I've ever actually talked to are the two we found at the bar at Bowman's Corner, where we used to drink during high school. Senior year we met there to watch the Super Bowl and the first thing we see, even before Joe Montana struggling with the Bengals, is two Hutterite kids, maybe our age. Never seen one in a bar before.

At first we just ignored them, but the owner kept us beered and pretty soon we asked him to bring the Hoots a round, on us. They weren't drinking and we just wanted to see what they'd do with a beer. What they did was bring their beers over and join us, saying, "Tank you wery much," and smiling. We could hardly believe it, but somebody managed to ask them what colony they're from, and which team they're for.

We talked about the game for a while and though I was curious about what went on in their colonies—simple stuff, like where they slept and where they ate, who had to do what chores—it seemed too rude just to ask. Pretty soon no one was saying anything and when out of the blue Carlton asked one if he'd trade his thick, home-stitched black coat for Carlton's perfectly good down jacket, it seemed like the funniest thing in the world.

The Hoot had smooth skin, white, and two red spots popped up like bruises on his cheeks. "Na, I coon't do dat," he says. After that, every time one of them would say anything one of us would answer, "Na, I coon't do dat," and we'd all laugh.

When San Francisco finally pulled it out at the end, the one with the white skin says, "Dat vus wan helluva game," smiling, trying to talk sports. Just like anyone.

Carlton shouts, "Na, I coon't do dat," and we all bust up laughing, though really it didn't make any sense and it was getting where it wasn't that funny anymore. But the Hoots keep smiling, like they're having a good time just being with regular people. Like they're one of us or something.

As they get up to go the other Hoot even tips his hat and says, "Tank you wery much," again. For the beer I suppose.

We all got up right after they did. There was maybe five of us. I don't remember exactly how it got going, but we caught them just as they were getting into their truck.

Sitting freezing on the haystacks I hear the elk moving in, their heart-shaped feet crunching over the brittle stubble, but I don't lift myself up. I try to remember how it started in the parking lot out front of Bowman's, but all I can remember is the squeal of the hard-packed snow under our boots, the clouds of our ragged breaths, and the huge ripping sound the black cloth of the Hoot's coat made. They weren't much for fighting and they were outnumbered as hell. We pounded on them until Carlton shouted, "Na, I coon't do dat!" as loud as he could, which was all of a sudden so funny we had to stop punching and kicking just to get our breath.

We watched them climb into their truck then, the white-skinned one behind the wheel, wiping at the blood beneath his nose with his torn, snow-covered sleeve. As they drove away, their truck's exhaust densely white in the cold air, we stood quietly in the parking lot, looking at the ground. The Hoots' blood was bright on the snow, and for a long time none of us said anything.

Then somebody, could've been me even, said, "I yust coon't do dat," but that wasn't funny at all anymore and without saying another word, or even looking at one another, we got into our trucks and drove home. It was dark by the time we reached our ranch. My knuckles stung like fire and I ground them into the thigh of my jeans. I wondered if back at their colony the Hoots would be able to explain what had happened. I would have liked to have heard.

Picturing the bright red drops of Hoot blood in the snow, so bright and so red it looked fake, I get up on my elbows, my rifle to my eye. I see the shapes of a whole herd spread out below me, dark ghosts against the crust of thin snow in the stubble. I even hear them starting to feed, the crunching grind of their big flat teeth. After watching them a second I hit the spotlight.

A whole field of glaring walleyes are caught in the light and the shapes of the closest jump out clear, with perfect hard black shadows etched into the snow behind them. I pick the closest elk. Caught in the sudden glare his eyes never waver. But the others break at the sound of the shot, and still thinking of the terrible brightness of the blood in the parking lot, I empty my rifle into the air, suddenly way madder about hay loss than makes sense.

When my rifle's empty, the barrel hot enough to burn, I look down at the lone dead elk, thrashing around, shot through the head. Carlton, I know, would have wiped out the whole herd, just for the good of the ranch.

I climb down and as I wait for the last kicks to die out, I try to remember if Carlton had really been with us when we thumped the Hoots. For years I was sure he had been, could see him breathing hard and punching right alongside me, but he's older than me and would've been long gone by then.

After gutting the elk I all of a sudden remember I'm freezing and instead of dragging him to the shop I go back to the house instead. The elk can always wait till morning.

I stoke up the wood stove and stand beside it a long time, my hands behind my back, tingling as they warm up. I stare at the yellow-painted kitchen table. I wonder what it would look like to have that Hoot girl sitting at it, staring at me, her eyes spotlight-bright with knowing what I'd done at Bowman's.

Before long I sit down and pull the pad of paper to me. I draw squiggles for a while. I wrote to Carlton a lot at first, but without him answering I gave it up. This is the first letter I've written since the one last year, letting him know Mom died.

I start out telling him I busted one of Mom's elk and it should make some dandy eating. It's something I think'll make him smile, and I smile myself thinking of the surprise of that gap-tooth grin. But I remember his next-to-final outrage: Mom and me walking into the shop to find him skinning out a young cow elk. Mom asked real quiet, "Where did that come from?" and just as quiet Carlton says, "The stacks. They're eating us alive." Then Mom was shouting about her pets and how he never acted this way when Dad was alive and Carlton went on working his knife as if she wasn't there. I went and sat on the front porch but I could still hear them, could hear Carlton finally yell, "Go ahead then! Starve!"

He came stomping by me on the porch and then a while later came stomping back out, carrying a big box he threw into the back of his pickup. He said, "See you, kid. You got any sense, you won't be far behind," still so mad he could barely talk.

I didn't realize then he was leaving for good, and nothing he said made sense. Us starve? We were surrounded by cattle. And me follow him? I was twelve years old.

I shake my head and pull my sheet of paper from the tablet and slip it into the stove. I butchered that elk myself. Mom wouldn't touch it. First time I ever butchered anything.

On a fresh sheet I ask Carlton if he was with us at Bowman's when we thumped the Hoots. I tell him I know he couldn't have been. I chew on the end of my pencil a minute, wondering who it could have been if it wasn't Carlton. But I haven't seen any of the high school gang since they blew town and none of their faces come to mind.

Next I ask if he ever really used to do that with the Hoot girls, through the sheets. I tell him I know he couldn't have done that either, but I say it's something I really got to know now. I tell him it's okay if he never did; I know how people talk, how lies like that aren't even lies so much as just a way of talking. So I tell him to just let me know the truth. You're so far away, I say, what difference would it make what I knew about you when we were just kids?

I close talking about the ranch, how I can't really run the whole thing alone, if I get down to admitting it. I don't ask him to come up or anything, but just leave it out there for him to look at. I figure there must be a world of things he looks at while he's out on the rigs with nothing but waves all around him. I lick the envelope and press the flap down with the side of my fist before I have a chance to put in anything about the pretty Hutterite girl, which is why I started the letter in the first place.

I pull some blankets from the closet then and a pillow from the arm of the couch and decide I'll head to town again in the morning, see if there's anything I might need at the hardware. The odds, I figure, of running into the same girl are awful slim, but maybe I'll stay in town all day, checking into the store now and then. I can't believe I bolted like I did when she smiled.

I stretch out on the kitchen bench and pull my blankets up tight to my neck, not wanting to leave the scorching heat of the stove just to drag myself to a cold bedroom. More and more often lately I sleep in the kitchen for just that reason.

I check the hardware store four times, but the Hutterite girl isn't in town the next day. I mail the letter to Carlton and in the next two weeks I start running into town more than ever before, burning up gas I can't afford. Every time I come home I look at the shop and tell myself I have to butcher that elk, but I keep thinking of Carlton's elk hanging in there and I put it off. It's cold enough it won't spoil.

Though I cover every place I've ever seen a Hutterite, I don't find the girl until the middle of December. She's at a craft thing downtown, at a table full of Hutterite women, selling hand-sewn stuff for Christmas presents. By the time I see her she's already seen me and this time I head to the table before I can think, before I realize she's never lowered her eyes, that she's still looking right at me.

"Hi," I say, wondering if she could really remember me.

She smiles, the same way she did at the store, and says, "Would you like someting." The accent's there, just like any Hoot, and I wonder what I could have been thinking.

"I'd like to know your name," I say anyway.

Not even a blush. The smile stays there and she says, "Amy." Amy, like somebody who sat next to you in kindergarten. I'd been expecting something like Gertrude or Wilhelmina.

An older woman sees me and starts my way and I say, "Where do you live?" and she says fast, "Goodhaven Colony."

Then the older woman is between us, squeezing the girl away from the table, saying, "Vut is it dat you vant?"

I see the girl, Amy, roll her pale eyes toward the ceiling, still smiling. Looking at the big Hoot woman I point at Amy and say, "Her."

Amy's smile actually breaks into a laugh and as the cluster of thick, short women grows she's bustled away and I'm told to "Shoo, shoo."

I shout my name to Amy, and, "I'm in the book," and I'm laughing myself by the time the men get there, milling around, hoping I'll leave them alone. One of them finally talks, mumbling about the hard times the girl is having now, her confusion. He smiles uncertainly and gives a shrug. "Forget dat girl," he says. "Stay vitch your own people."

I think of her smile and I say, quiet enough he won't hear, "I yust coon't do dat."

I know where Goodhaven Colony is, but, driving out of town, the light fading fast, I know I can't just drive into the colony and ask her to a show or something. Out there, outnumbering me a hundred to one, I wonder how peaceable they'd be.

I park by the back door but night is full on me and I sit in the pickup, listening to the radio, knowing it's cold and empty inside the house. Eventually I dash in and fire up the stove. I listen to the crackling of the kindling and add bigger stuff, then decide to head out and butcher the elk, which I've put off way too long already.

I unlock the shop door and find the elk frozen solid. I slap at him, wondering how I'm going to butcher something as hard as bone. I get into my coveralls and wrestle with the little bull for an hour just to get the skin off. I take a breather then and ask the naked elk if he thinks they have phones at the colonies. "Hello, is Amy there?" I say to the carcass. "Amy who? Amy the pretty one. Amy the confused one." I grin, but begin to admit I don't have a chance.

I cut the elk into front and back halves with a handsaw but it's tough going. Getting impatient, I crank up a chain saw to split him lengthwise along the spine. Curls and chips of meat and bone flick against my coveralls, but as the saw heats up it starts melting things and blood begins to stain the floor.

I'm making a mess and losing every trace of hope I'd had at the craft show. I can't believe how far I've sunk on my own—tearing up an elk with a chain saw just because I've been mooning after some impossible Hoot while the pet elk I poached freezes hard as a statue.

I flip the saw off and when the chain stops rotating I give it a kick. The saw scuttles across the bloody concrete floor and I'm left standing over the pieces of frozen elk. A voice behind me says, "Drew?"

I spin around but before I even see him in the doorway I know it's Carlton. He smiles a little, seeing my surprise, but it doesn't cover the shock on his face. "I got your letter," he says. "I figured you could use a hand."

I jump over to the door, sticking out my hand, but Carlton backs into the darkness, holding up his hands to keep me away. I stop, startled again, but glancing down I see that the chain saw has sprayed me up and down with melted elk stuff. "Let me get this off," I say, starting to strip out of the coveralls. "I was just butchering up . . . ," I start, but Carlton's seen what I was doing. The shop is a wreck.

I unzip the coveralls so fast the zipper sticks and I have to wriggle out. I throw them toward the band saw but instead of catching, the coveralls slip to the floor. I leave them there and leap through the black hole of the door where Carlton had been just a moment before.

"Carlton?" I say.

"Right here," he answers, from over by the truck.

As I crunch over the frozen ground I say, "I'm cleaned up now," and I see him against the light from the house and we shake hands.

We stand there a minute, though the night's cold as can be. "I got up here and couldn't find you anywhere," Carlton says.

I still haven't let go of his hand and Carlton continues, "I've called every night since I left Texas."

"Texas," I say, trying to imagine being there so long and then suddenly back here.

"It's darker than the inside of a cow out here," Carlton says, pulling away from me and heading for the house. "What happened to the yard light?"

It burned out months ago. I try laughing. "I leave it off to save money," I say.

"Thin times?" he asks and I catch his accent, Southern and slow, and as we head to the house I kid him about it.

We step inside, into the light, and Carlton shrugs and says, "Lived there my whole adult life, Drew." He backs up to the stove and looks over his shoulder. "Can't afford fuel oil?"

"We still got oil," I say. "I just like the wood."

"You'll get over that when the pipes burst," he drawls.

We stand beside the stove with our backs to each other. I hadn't thought of freezing the pipes. "How long you been here?" I ask, looking around the kitchen, at my pillow and pile of blankets on the bench. I wonder what in the world he thinks.

"I've been here for a while," he answers, "waiting for you to show up. I never thought to look in the shop."

He doesn't say anything else so I ask, right out, "What are you doing here, Carlton?"

"I got your letter, like I said."

There's more he's going to say, but he doesn't, so I turn and creak open the stove doors, shoving in a new log and then another. I have to push the second one in and beat on it to get the doors closed again.

"For the record, Drew," Carlton says to my back, "that wasn't me with you at Bowman's."

I stand up and smile at him. "No," I say, "I knew it couldn't've been."

"What did you pound a couple of Hutterite kids for?"

I shrug. Coming from him, it's a pretty dumb question. He was always fighting somebody. "They were Hoots," I say.

Carlton looks as if he still doesn't understand, as if he somehow feels sorry for me, and I ask, "What did you screw them through the sheets for?"

Carlton looks at his feet. "That was just talk," he says. "Punk kids trying to look tough. Nobody ever did anything like that."

I look at him sideways and his grin comes back, sudden and surprising as ever, making me smile. "Till you said that in your letter I'd forgotten what an asshole I used to be."

My smile dies out. "What are you talking about?"

"We should have a drink," he says, all of a sudden loud and cheerful. "How long's it been since we've seen each other?"

"Not since you blew out of here," I say. "Nine years."

Carlton whistles. "Well, where's the booze? Come on."

I see he's trying hard to sound like his old self and I dip beneath the sink and set a bottle of whiskey on the table. Carlton wipes at the dust on the bottle and laughs. I interrupt, saying, "It's left over from Mom's funeral. I think the Waldners brought that bottle over."

Carlton isn't laughing anymore and I get glasses. We sit at the yellow table and Carlton pours for each of us. "Nine years, eh? Last time I saw you, you were nothing but a pimply-faced kid. Thirteen? Fourteen?"

"Twelve," I say.

"Twelve then," he answers, holding up his glass for me to click mine against. I realize what a tiny part of his life I must have always been.

"So tell me," Carlton says, "what'd you grow up to be?" Without waiting for an answer he shakes his head. "Pounding Hoots in the bars. Massacring elk with a chain saw. You a tough guy?"

"You were more than tough enough for this family," I say.

He keeps shaking his head and I ask, "What did you grow up to be?" really curious, not just filling up silence like he was. He talks like I was from another planet, instead of just trying to fill his shoes.

"I grew up to be married," he says, sipping and hiding behind his glass at the same time.

I stare at him and he nods.

"Divorced?" I ask, thinking now I know why he's here.

Carlton shakes his head. "Not in a million years. She's a keeper."

I look around the table for my glass.

"She's back in Texas looking after the kids," he tells me.

For a last time I picture Carlton out on the rigs surrounded by waves, only now I see that he probably never once thought about me or Mom or any of the things I pictured him thinking about. He was out there thinking about his own new family the whole time. "Kids?" I say.

"Two. Jen and Olive."

"Olive," I say, like a parrot. Our Mom's name.

"Horrible thing to do to a kid, isn't it? Sounds like she's a hundred years old."

I watch Carlton stand up to add more wood to the stove that's still stoked to bursting. He gazes into the open doors, the heat glowing against his face. "How old's Olive?" I ask.

"Two," he says and thumps the stick there's no room for against the floor.

"Mom was alive then. I suppose you could've told her. At least that you were married."

"You could suppose that," he says. The doors squeal as he closes them. "But things like that got to seem harder than maybe they really were."

I can't do anything but stare at him, wondering who he is.

"Anyway," he says, "I came up to see if you'd lost the place yet. Or if you'd driven it so far into the hole it wasn't ever coming back. If it looks all right we're hoping to all come up to stay. What do you think?"

If *I'd* lost it, I think, if *I'd* driven it into a hole. I say, "What I think, Carlton, is it probably wasn't much to sit out in the waves and collect oil wages. You want to try to run this place alone, have at it. See how far out of the hole you take it!" I'm shouting, but Carlton had worried about frozen pipes right off and I know I'm not making sense.

"I didn't mean it that way," he says, tossing his stick back into the box. I wish he'd just smack me, like he would have when we were kids.

"What I meant was I'm thinking of coming back, with my family. Giving this place another go. With you."

I think of the cattle out there now, hunched up in the draws against the cold and the dark. "You can't just give it a go," I say.

"I'd be in for everything, Drew. This is where I want my kids to grow."

"I can see that," I say. "I mean, after the bang up job of growing you did here."

Carlton stares at me and I say, "You're a piece of work, Carlton, you know that? Remember your goddamn elk?"

I stare back at him.

"What in the world did you make up down there? What kind of kid did you invent for yourself to be?"

I'm shouting again and I stop suddenly and get up. "Olive!" I snort, and I walk across the house because I don't know what to say next and I don't want him to see how hard I'm shaking.

I snag a coat on my way out and storm straight ahead, going nowhere until I cut the footprints in the snow crust. There's just enough moon for me to see their snaky path heading up the hill. I kneel down to make sure, but I know they're Carlton's. I haven't been up to the hill since the last snow, since I popped Mom's elk.

I fall into Carlton's track. It's a hike and I'm blowing clouds by the time I can see the fence around the stones. Carlton's tracks go straight through, the gate closed neatly over them.

I work the latch and follow Carlton's steps around the whole collection; Mom and Dad, and Mom's parents, and her baby sister's little spot. Carlton's tracks are shuffled around Dad's grave but in front of Mom's there are two long icy grooves, like the spots elk melt into the snow when they bed down, only much smaller.

I kneel down to study them and before I'm even all the way down I realize they're the prints of Carlton's knees, down long enough he melted through. Thinking back to him standing in the bright light of the shop door I can see him perfectly, can see the darkness around his knees, the white, crusty snow sticking to his pants around the edges of the wet.

I feel the cold working into my knees, stiffening them, and I say, "What the hell, Mom?" It's not something to say to someone I don't doubt is in heaven, but I say it again. I picture them fighting over his elk and I hear again the sudden, short chop of Carlton shouting, "Go ahead then! Starve!" and I hear Mom the next morning, even after his final outrage, saying, "We're going to miss him, Drew," and I realize I don't have any idea what there was between them. But, just as suddenly, I know it wasn't Carlton at Bowman's that day. It was me, pretending.

When I get up, I leave the gate open for the elk, though there's precious little left there for them now.

At the kitchen door I'm staggered by the great heat of the overloaded stove. "Carlton?" I say, before my eyes adjust to the light. There's no answer.

By the time I go through the last room I'm running. The house is empty again. I step back outside and his truck is still beside mine. I lean against it and take a big breath. In the quiet blackness of the night the cold pinches my skin. And then I hear the familiar thin whine of butchering coming from the shop.

I bang the shop door shut behind me so Carlton will know I'm there. He's at the band saw and he peeks over his shoulder, still pushing a piece of the frozen elk through the whirring blade. "That's a good way to lose a finger," I say, which is what he always used to say to me when I tried to help.

He drops a chop into a box on the floor beside him, a box that's already full. He's nearly through the spine and he turns back to the saw to push the last cuts through. The bone smokes a little and the smell is terrible and the whining scream worsens until the blade is back into meat. I haven't kept the blades sharp.

Carlton drops the last cut into the box and switches off the saw. The blade wobbles as it slows and the scream is gone, which I'm glad for. Just as the blade slows to where I can see each individual sharklike tooth, Carlton says, "That's my coat."

I look down and see that I'm wearing his old lineman's jacket, what he used to call his shit-kicking coat. "First thing I grabbed," I say, though I've been wearing it for years, since before the fight at Bowman's.

Carlton's got the blower on high and I hear the first clump of ice drop from the knees of my jeans. "Did you call your wife?" I ask.

Carlton shakes his head. "I was going to," he says. "Even had my hand on the phone, but I thought I better wait, see if we can really talk it over."

"Nothing to talk over," I say. "Everything here's as much yours as it is mine."

Carlton shakes his head again. "Not with the way things've gone."

"Why?" I start, but my voice shakes. "Why didn't you come back when there was still time?"

Carlton wipes some meat and bone from the saw table. "What did Mom call them?"

"Your outrages," I answer, knowing exactly what he's talking about.

"Outrages," he says, rolling the word around as he nods his head. "Outrages," he says again. "After that last one . . ." He lets the words fade between us as he stands in my coveralls, polishing that old saw table with the sleeve.

When everything is long silent, Carlton looks up again, his grin cracking open. "What say we go back in and finish that drink. We can both call home. Give them the good news."

Home, I think. "Can't," I say. "I got a date."

"A date?" Carlton asks, his smile growing wider, more friendly than I ever remember it.

"Yeah," I answer. I glance at my watch. "I got to meet her at nine. At the farmer's market." It's the wrong thing to say, but right then it's the only place I picture seeing a Hutterite.

Carlton watches me. "There's no farmer's market in December," he says.

"Just a place she knows," I say.

He glances me up and down. "You're going like that?"

I nod. "She won't mind."

"Must be quite a girl."

I nod again.

"Does she have a name?"

"Amy."

I see him thinking, going over the neighbors' places, trying to picture some little girl from back in his day. "She's not from around here," I tell him.

"A foreigner, huh?"

"She's from Goodhaven," I say, studying the blood on the coveralls, as if I stared at the splotches long enough I'd be able to read our futures.

"Goodhaven?" he repeats, like the name rings some bells.

"Goodhaven Colony. She's not a foreigner. She's a Hutterite."

I can feel Carlton looking at me. "A Hoot?"

"Maybe you know her," I say, unable to help myself. "Maybe she's one you did through the sheets."

Carlton looks me in the eye a long time, then takes a big,

careful breath. "I told you," he says, "that never happened. To any-body."

"You told me a lot of things," I say.

It's been dark for hours by the time I cruise through the va-cant parking lot where they hold the farmer's market in summer. I've got the brights on and I drive to sweep them around, but there's no one there. Carlton's back home, already in his old room. He hasn't called his wife yet, but the yard light was working when I pulled out. He waved from the door and told me to have a good time, and I wonder now what I'm going to tell him.

I make up a story about Amy getting caught, about how at this very moment she's locked in a room somewhere in the colony, the door barricaded by German men all in black. But, though I've made this all up, I start to get the hollow feeling I've been stood up—that Hoots can probably be just as mean as us.

I park and turn off the lights and then the engine. I roll down the window to let the cold in. A few cars make their way past, grinding over the ice in the street, but it's a pretty quiet night.

The cab light flashes on when I open my door and I close it quick to be back in the dark. I walk through the lot, picturing the boxes of baby potatoes and long zucchinis, the giant loaves of bread the Hutterites sell.

I catch a glimpse of someone slipping through the light by the street, a thin blade of a person, walking fast, toward me, and for an instant I think this could actually all come true. But the person hustles on, not swerving an inch my way before disappearing around the corner.

I walk back to the truck and sit down, slicked with sweat from that instant of fear, but with the cold sinking deep inside my clothes, inside my bones. I think again of Carlton at the ranch, of the pipes that'll never freeze, and I turn the engine over, listen to its cranky roar.

After Carlton left us that day—after he'd shouted, "Go ahead then! Starve!"—Mom and I'd skittered around each other in the big house like it was us that'd had the fight, instead of her and Carlton. I went to bed early just to get away from it. Then I lay in the dark, looking at all the new empty filling my room without Carlton. That's how I heard the shots, a lot of them, hot and fast, and I knew Carlton was still out there somewhere in the dark, killing things.

I don't know if Mom heard or not.

All night I waited for him to come back, and I snuck downstairs before it even got light, still in my pajamas. The kitchen was cold and I shivered, but I decided Carlton really was gone, and that from now on I'd have to give Mom more of a hand. I started the fire in the stove, and got out the coffee. It wasn't till I was getting the water for the pot that I saw what Carlton had done. His final outrage.

The only light on in the house, the one I'd turned on when I reached the kitchen, was just strong enough to cut through the glary old glass of the sink window. Carlton must've known that. It lit the head of the elk he'd hung from the porch rafters, hung so it'd stare inside the house, stare in at Mom making coffee, which was how every other day had always started here. The elk eyes were already sunken and gray, not shiny black or alive, and its tongue dangled out like something obscene. Its little spike horns looked like the devil's, and I jumped back, my heart oilcanning, quick bile burning my throat.

I went outside without even grabbing a coat, barefooting over the crunching frost to the shop for a ladder so I could get the elk head down before Mom found what Carlton had done. But, once on the ladder, I couldn't get the come-along to let loose, even beating on it with my numb fists.

I ran back inside, breathing hard, like I was barely holding back from crying, and I threw on Carlton's jacket for the first time, his shit-kicking coat, and stepped into a pair of rubber overboots two sizes too big for me. I dashed back out to the shop, judging the coming of day by the strip of gray edging the horizon, and I moved even faster, tripping in the big boots, needing to get this done before Mom got up, needing to do that more than I'd ever needed anything in my life.

Grabbing a hammer I made it back up the ladder and I beat on the come-along release until there was the sudden quick shriek of whistling cable and the flat *thwap* of the head striking the planks of the porch, the wood-on-wood sound of the antlers. It rocked the ladder, and I hung tight for an instant before starting the careful descent in my clumsy shoes. That's when I saw Mom, tousled from the bed, like she hadn't slept any more than I had. She stood in the center of the kitchen, in her bathrobe, far away from the counters, from anything she could grab for support. She was watching me.

I didn't know how much she'd seen, so before going in I rolled the head off the porch, hoping I could get it away before Mom left the house. But as soon as I walked through the door, Mom held her arms open for me and when I stepped into them she held me tight, and I said, "He didn't mean it, Mom."

Mom kept tisking at how cold I was, like I hadn't said a thing, but she stopped dead then, only running her fingers down the seams of the coat she had just noticed was Carlton's. "We're going to miss him, Drew," she said, her voice shivery. "We'll just have to do our best without him."

And that's when, I realize at last, I'd decided I'd do my best at being both of us instead.

I blow out a big breath that fogs the windshield, then back out of the empty farmer's market without looking over my shoulder, knowing there's nothing behind me I could possibly damage. I start down the strip, falling into the cruising line of the few high schoolers waiting for something to happen.

I figure Carlton's calling his wife. Soon his whole family will be living at the ranch and the yard will always be brightly lit and the elk will be pets again. I figure sometime soon, before spring, I'll call and tell Carlton not to mow the graves, so Mom can have the elk up there with her.

In front of me the high schoolers are turning around, starting back the way they came. I rub my face and when it's my turn at the end of the drag, instead of turning around, I keep going. In a minute I'm out of town altogether, the whole world black except for the tiny spot inside my headlights.

I play out the run of road ahead of me. Not too far ahead is the section road cutting off toward Goodhaven, where the pretty Hoot lives with all those grim men in black, those big women in their polka dots.

Beyond that is everything else, even, I figure, Texas. With no idea which turn I'll take, I wonder if this is the same way Carlton went.

d r y RAIN

With one hand clamped on Joey's forehead, Stil shouts into the phone, "What? What?" He locks his elbow, keeping Joey a full arm's length away.

Joey yells, "Just let me talk to her! I'll tell her it's okay!"

"*What?*" Stil bellows into the ancient phone, a rotary dial for Christ's sake, like Canada's some third-world country.

"I'm okay, Mom!" Joey shouts. "We're having fun."

Slashing the phone to his side, the booth rattling as the cable hits its limit, Stil hisses to Joey, "Would you? For one second?"

Joey quits shouting and Stil wraps his hand around the top of his head, hauling him into the booth, a finger on one temple, a thumb on the other. He presses Joey's face against his ribs, then carefully lifts the phone back to his ear. "Now, Tracy," he says, shouting again, "you were saying what?"

Stil listens.

"You *do* owe me!" he roars. "I had a life with you! You owe me for that!"

Suddenly Stil pulls the phone away from his ear, stares at it, clamps it back to his head. Dead. Hung up. He stares at it again, then slams it against the box on the wall.

The phone breaks neatly in half and Stil stops, already halfway out of the booth, having always pictured himself hanging up on her just that way, but thinking it was impossible; phones made of something from NASA or someplace, something that could tolerate reentry, splashdown.

When he looks down, Joey's head is no longer pinched beneath his hand. Joey's out in the street, holding the black earpiece of the phone, shouting into it, "What? What? *What?*"

Stil smiles shakily. "Get out of the street," he says, though he guesses you'd have a better chance getting hit by lightning than by a car in this speck of town.

Hopping onto the sidewalk, Joey wallops the booth with his piece of phone. "What?" he yells.

Stil fingers the change in his pocket, American coins, and not many of them, two bucks maybe. This is all taking longer than he'd supposed.

The day's blazing, and Stil pulls his shirt away from his skin. Beyond the single street, the few stores, the post office, they're surrounded by nothing but fields. Thunderheads loom tall in the hazy sun, rain smearing from their bottoms, maybe reaching the tabletop of land, but probably sizzling out before getting the chance.

"Virga," Joey says.

Stil looks at him. "What?"

"Virga," Joey says. "That's what it's called. When the rain can't reach the ground."

Stil glances from his son to the clouds and back. "It's just dry rain," he says. "Depressing as hell."

Joey looks a second longer. "I like it," he says.

Then, turning away from the sky, Joey taps the phone on his thigh. "What did Mom say?" he asks.

Stil watches the rain going nowhere. "How would I know?" he answers. "Couldn't hear a word with your howling. Could've been a wrong number for all I heard."

"What'd she say?" Joey says again.

Stil stares down at his boy. He rattles the change in his pocket. Two bucks, he thinks. "Is there something you haven't told me?" he asks at last. "Something about your ears?"

"I hear everything," Joey answers.

A shiver wracks Stil's shoulders. He pulls his hand out of his pocket. "Let's get something to eat. What do you figure they eat up here anyway?"

"Grass," Joey says.

Stil smiles. The whole place does smell like cut grass, some gigantic golf course; wheat or hay or whatever they grow. "Can people eat grass?" he asks.

"If they're hungry enough," Joey answers. He looks at his phone and yells, "What?" into it. "*Mom?*"

"Knock it off," Stil says.

In the cafe Stil stares at his change. Two dollars and forty-four cents. There are a few damp bills in his wallet. "We're rich," he says to Joey.

Tracy has all the money in the world. Stil knows that. All she has to do is share. Stil wonders if she has a warrant out; if the border guys will nab him as soon as they see Joey yelling "What?" into his chunk of phone.

They're the only people in the cafe and it's a while before a waitress peeks out from the back. Stil whispers, "Put that thing away," and Joey hides the phone beneath the table.

"American money?" Stil asks as the waitress approaches.

"This is America, too," she answers.

"U.S."

She looks at them. "Sure," she says. "Straight across."

A thirty-percent hit on the exchange. "Can't keep this up long," he says to Joey.

Joey shrugs. He bangs the phone on the bottom of the table and the waitress jumps.

"*What?*" Joey yells.

Stil shakes his head. "It's been kind of a big day for him," he explains. He orders a hamburger.

The waitress tilts her head toward Joey.

"We'll split it," Stil says, and the waitress edges away.

"You want to get us arrested?" Stil whispers to Joey.

Joey opens his mouth to shout "What?" but Stil stops him.

"Take it easy," Stil says. "Mom might've misunderstood all this. She might've called the cops. We got to play it cool."

"But . . ."

"But quit acting like a loon," Stil interrupts.

Joey lifts his phone to his ear, whispers, "Now, you were saying what?"

Stil shakes his head. "A parrot," he says. "A fucking mynah bird." He apologizes for swearing.

Joey shrugs.

"We'll call again after lunch," Stil says. "Find a phone that wasn't personally installed by Alexander Graham Bell."

The waitress sets the burger in the center of the table and scurries away. Only one plate.

"How much are you trying to get for me?" Joey asks.

Stil takes time cutting the burger in two. He lifts the bigger side in his hand. "It's not like that," he says, shaking a big loop of ketchup onto the meat. "I told you before."

"You get me out of school," Joey recites. "We cross into Canada. You call Mom. You call her three times. You never call Mom."

Stil, with his mouth full, says, "Eat your burger."

"I like cheese."

Stil rolls his eyes and calls for the waitress. "He wants cheese on his," he explains.

"On just the half?"

Stil shrugs. "He's on vacation."

The waitress whisks up the plate.

"Melted," Joey says, shaking half a phone at her.

Stil gives him a little smile and the waitress retreats.

"This is like gangsters," Joey says. "Mom'd kill me."

"Just take it easy," Stil answers. "Before the Mounties surround us."

Joey laughs.

"What's so funny?" Stil says, setting the last bite of his burger down on the bare table and wiping his mouth. "Could happen."

The waitress returns Joey's half and he studies the melted cheese. "What're we going to do next?" he asks.

"We got to call again."

"About the money," Joey says. It's not a question. He stuffs the last of his cheeseburger into his mouth. "We should rob a bank."

Stil can barely understand him around his mouthful. He eyes his boy as he chews, always forgetting how sharp he is. He wonders where in the world that came from. Not from him, that's for sure. Not from his mother. Some kind of freak of nature.

"So, you like living in the Big Sky?" Stil asks, trying not to remember sitting slumped in his car watching the huge house, the grassy cuts of the ski runs behind it, the lawyer and his kids coming and going, Tracy; Joey's whole new family.

"It's okay," Joey answers. "Not as bad as you think."

"What makes you think I think it's bad?"

"You hate lawyers," Joey says.

Stil rolls his eyes, but Joey keeps pressing. "We're in Canada, Dad. We're making ransom calls."

"Now, goddamn it, Joey, I did not kidnap you." Stil tries to keep it down, but he's shouting a whisper. "I told you that. You're my kid. We're supposed to do things like this. It's good for you."

"You didn't even get visitation, Dad."

"Only lawyers worry about that crap."

"Lawyers and cops."

"Same thing," Stil answers, looking out at the blistering street. He remembers playing with tar bubbles in the road on days like this and he asks Joey if he ever does that.

"What kind of bubbles?" Joey asks.

"Never mind," Stil says. He stands up, checks his wallet for the last of the bills, fewer of those than he'd hoped, too. "Let's go."

"To call Mom?"

Stil asks the waitress where he could find a pay phone. She holds out his change, pointing vaguely down the block. Stil wonders if she's already called the Mounties, if they really wear those goofy red uniforms.

When Stil dials this time, Joey is quiet, waiting just outside the booth. While the phone rings, he pokes his head in long enough to say, "A hundred thousand. At least."

Stil reaches to push him out, and as his hand clamps around his head, his soft, thin hair, Joey squawks, "Well, I'm worth it, right?"

"You're not kidnapped," Stil says. "Jesus . . ."

"Then take me home," Joey dares.

"We're on vacation," Stil hisses. "That's all."

Tracy interrupts then, her voice fuzzy but just as daring as Joey's when she says, "Vacation my ass. You want to know what the FBI thinks of that theory?"

"Tracy," Stil says.

"You're talking to them right now," she says. "Every call's being recorded. What in the world are you doing in Canada?"

Stil's shirt has long since been soaked through in the heat, but now it's different, the smell of fear changing everything. Canada could be a guess. Last time she hung up on him. She wouldn't do that if the FBI were tracing the calls. But Stil knows Tracy can do anything, FBI or no.

"I just want what's coming to me, Trace."

"Coming to you! For what? Child support?"

Stil thinks. "Vacations aren't cheap," he says.

He listens to her deep, tired sigh. "You're broke, aren't you?"

"We don't have enough to come home," Stil admits. He can't stand how good it is to hear her.

He hears another voice in the background, a deep rumble. The FBI, or just the lawyer, getting impatient.

"Trace," Stil says, "you didn't really call the cops? The FBI?"

"Bring him back, Stil," Tracy answers. "Think of him, would you?"

Stil glances at Joey, standing outside the scratched glass, his piece of phone clamped to his ear, straining to hear.

And, as if he does hear every word, Joey suddenly yells, "We're having fun, Mom! I am!"

"He's enjoying it," Stil whispers.

"For God's sake, Stil."

"He is. You should see him."

"That's exactly what I want."

"Me too," Stil says, even more quietly.

"Bring him back and this is over, Stil. All forgotten. But I swear to God, if you ever touch him again . . ."

"I had a life," Stil says, cutting her off. He has to look away from Joey. "It's eye-for-an-eye time now, Trace." This time he hangs up on her, letting her chew on that until he finds another phone.

He steps out of the booth, waving for Joey to follow. "We got to hit the bricks, kid," he says.

"Is she tracing the calls? Are they closing in?"

When haven't they been, Stil thinks. But he says, "Vacation, Joey. They don't trace calls for a vacation."

Joey stops, looking close at Stil. "My school is for gifted, Dad," he says. "Not gimpy."

"I know, Joey." Stil opens the car door and waits for Joey to scoot across. "You just don't know anything about this."

"Then tell me."

"I don't know anything about it either," Stil answers.

Joey buckles his belt. He lifts his phone to his ear, then switches it to his mouth, whispering, "I had a life."

"Don't you ever say that," Stil snaps. "Not ever." He yanks at the key and they pull onto the road, heading west, back toward the mountains, the beautiful lives beneath the ski hill. He's paralleling the border, staying as close as he can.

She has to cave at the next call, Stil thinks. He glances at the map on the seat, deciding they'll cross over at Chief Mountain, drive through the park like a real vacation. Joey'll be home in time for Tracy to tuck him in.

She couldn't have called the FBI.

Stil glances at Joey. He's finally let go of the phone. It sits on the map between them, the broken end sharp and pointed like a quick, homemade weapon; a jagged beer bottle held at your throat. "Think of him," she'd said.

Stil rubs at his temples.

As the road climbs they leave the wheat country and its dry storms behind. The air blowing through the windows cools slightly.

"It's nice up here," Stil says, his voice scratchy. They haven't spoken in a long time. He clears his throat. "Smells good."

"Pine trees," Joey answers, staring out the window. "Conifers. Pine, spruce, fir, hemlock, cedar."

"Smells like one of those deodorizers."

Joey grins.

Stil makes himself smile. "How do you like that? Living in a place that smells like a giant Christmas tree hanging off your dash?"

Joey keeps smiling. After a while he asks, "Where do you live now, Dad?"

"I got a place," Stil says, so fast it sounds like a lie even to him. "Not far from where we all lived."

"In the desert?"

"On the edge."

"Never smells like this?"

Stil looks at his wrist crooked over the steering wheel. "No," he says.

They drive miles more and Stil asks, "You ever miss Arizona?"

"Mom calls it Bedrock. Like the Flintstones."

Stil nods. "Bedrock," he whispers. Their whole lives turned into a cartoon. He pushes his wind-blasted hair back flat on his head and pulls onto the shoulder, the smell of the pines everywhere.

Joey looks at him, wondering, and looking away from his eyes, Stil sees that Joey's shoes have pictures of Batman on the sides.

What the hell would Batman do now? Stil wonders. Probably *Kapow*! the hell out of him and fly Joey back to his mother.

"You like Batman?" he whispers.

Joey shrugs. "He's okay."

"When I was a kid it was Superman. He was everybody's favorite."

"He died," Joey says.

Stil can't look at the little shoes. He glances out the cracked side window. "Are you ten yet?" he asks.

Joey looks down at his bare knees. He moves the point of the phone in tiny circles against his skin. "Almost," he says.

"What do you think we should do?" Stil asks.

Joey puts the phone to his ear. "I can't hear you."

Stil says it again.

"What do you mean?" Joey asks.

"I mean right now. Jesus, I'm driving around Canada with a genius and I'm trying to figure everything out myself."

"I'm not smart about everything," Joey says with an apologetic shrug.

"You like that school?"

Joey scrunches his face. "School?" he asks.

A motor home lumbers by, real vacationers. "Man, we used to have some knockdowns about that," Stil says. "Me and your mom. I just wanted to let you be a kid, you know. But she was accelerated this, accelerated that."

Joey picks at a tear in the seat vinyl.

"You remember the first day you came home from the special classes? Goddamn, you couldn't've been six years old. You told us you quit. You said, 'It's supposed to be accelerated, not excessive.'"

Stil laughs. "I about busted a gut, but Mom got you all turned around. Marched you right back the next day."

"It wasn't that bad," Joey whispers.

"Well you're definitely the thinker here, pal. What should we do?"

"Mom won't give you any money for me?" Joey says, his voice so small Stil has to lean close to hear.

"Joey," Stil starts, but then takes a big breath. "I need the money," he admits. "I'm busted flat."

"But that's not why I got you," he goes on. "I did that just to show her. Just to show her what she did to me."

Joey picks up the phone. He holds the unbroken half to his mouth. "Did you even try to keep me? Get visitation?" He flips the phone around, the good half to his ear now, waiting.

Stil shifts behind the wheel. He puts his hand on the stick, his foot on the gas. But then he slumps low, the same position he'd watched Joey's new house from, watched him walk out to school alone, the lawyer's kids older.

"Not then," Stil says. "I couldn't right then."

Joey nods, the phone clamped to his ear.

"I wanted to," Stil begins fast, but Joey turns the phone around to speak into it.

Stil stops to hear him whisper, "I had a life with you. You owe me for that."

Stil glances quickly out the window. He begins to say, "Don't say that," but instead drops the car into drive and creeps back onto the pavement. They drive along, Joey whispering into the phone; words Stil can't and doesn't want to hear.

"You want to go to Arizona with me?" he asks at last.

Joey looks up. Into the phone he says, "We'd starve, Dad."

Stil tries to smile. "We could eat grass."

"There's no grass in Arizona."

"On the golf courses."

"We'd never get memberships."

Stil looks down the highway. "I suppose not," he says. "Not to eat the grass."

Joey doesn't play along, and taking a big breath, Stil asks, "You want me to take you back to your mom's house?"

Joey shrugs. "It's where I live now," he whispers. He looks out the side window, away from Stil. Raising his voice just loud enough, he says, "I'll make her give you some money."

"Ah," Stil says, lifting his hand to wave off the offer, but he doesn't say anything else. He needs the money.

Stil drives faster than he should, especially if she's got a warrant out for him. He stops at one more phone, making Joey stay in the car while he talks to Tracy. When he gets back in, Joey wants to know what they said, but Stil doesn't say a word. He drives even faster, trying to make the roar of wind so loud he won't be able to hear Joey asking again and again about what they'd said; what they'd decided about him.

Not until the sign says they're approaching the border does Stil slow to a crawl. As soon as he sees the tidy white custom buildings he pulls over, then backs up, out of sight. Immediately he wishes he hadn't done that, imagining nothing looking more suspicious.

He shuts off the car, to hear better if anyone comes at him. Then he turns to Joey. "Really," he starts, "Joey. I wasn't kidnapping you. I just wanted to show her."

Joey nods. "Just to show her," he says into the phone.

Stil closes his eyes for an instant. "That's not what I mean," he starts.

But Joey lowers the phone from his ear, not listening. He begins widening the rip in the vinyl, digging into it with the hard point of the broken end of the phone.

"I'm not going back with you, Joey. I can't cross the border right here."

"It's a vacation, Dad. They don't alert the borders for a vacation."

"Yeah, well, maybe she misunderstood."

"Yeah," Joey answers. "Maybe she did."

Stil opens his door and Joey does the same. They meet in front of the car.

"Mom's on her way," Stil says. "She's going to pick you up here."

Joey peels a broken grasshopper off the grille. He pulls off a wing. "Is she bringing the money?"

Stil looks down at the top of his son's head. "No," he says. "I don't think so."

"I'll send you some. Do you have an address?"

"I'll write. Let you know."

Joey glances up. "You never write, Dad."

"Well, I will now."

"For the money."

"No. For you. So you can write back. Tell me about that rain. That vertigo."

"Dry rain, Dad. Vertigo's something totally different."

Stil nods, picturing the drops starting out like regular rain, but burning up, then just gone. "Maybe Mom will let you come down to see me sometime," he says.

"Mom?" Joey says. He laughs.

"I suppose not," Stil answers. He brushes back his hair, his hands empty and useless.

Stil glances down the quiet road. "You shouldn't have to wait too long. She should be here soon."

Joey nods. "Did she really call the police on us?"

"I don't know. She says she did."

"She might have," Joey says.

Stil shrugs.

"Well, you better go then. Before the Mounties get here."

"Yeah." Stil kneels on the edge of the road beside his son. He puts his arm quickly around Joey, though they've never done much touching.

As Joey leans into him, resting the top of his head against Stil's cheek, Stil notices the tar webbing the road, thick bands of patching filling the cracks.

"Watch this," he whispers into his son's ear, and letting Joey go, he reaches down, pressing his finger into a swelling blister of hot tar.

The tar bulges away from his touch and he presses another finger beside it. Finally the bubble is trapped between his fingers and a block of solid tar. It pops, a slow-motion balloon, leaking and settling back to the ground.

"Cool," Joey whispers.

"Sometimes you can lift out whole pieces, like rope."

"What do you do with them?"

Stil can't remember. He sees himself running through the streets of Phoenix, a lifetime ago, carrying a thick rope of hot road tar like a trophy. "Chase people with it, I guess."

"Who would I chase?"

"Your friends," Stil says, but he sees Joey walking out of the gigantic house by himself, his books in a heavy pack on his back, his head down, maybe looking for cracks, careful where he puts his feet, not breaking his mother's back.

Joey presses the toe of his Batman shoe against another bubble. It pops immediately. "Mom'd kill me for playing in the street," he says.

"Yeah, well," Stil answers.

Joey looks at his collapsing tar pocket. "She might be here already," he says. "I better go."

He lifts his hand just enough to graze it along Stil's. With his other hand he lifts the phone to his mouth. He's starting away when he asks, "Will you come back for another vacation?"

"You bet," Stil says, thinking what an awful wager that'd make.

Joey's walking away then.

"Joey," Stil calls. "Maybe you could," he starts, then falters. "Why don't you come to Arizona with me now? We could work something out with . . ."

Joey interrupts, raising his voice so he doesn't have to turn around. "I'll learn how to play with the tar before you come back, Dad," he shouts. "I'll know how."

"You bet," Stil whispers, his air leaking out as Joey walks away. Then he remembers. "Virga!" he shouts. "That's what it's called, Joey!"

Joey still doesn't turn around, only nods, and Stil slides behind the wheel onto the sun-hot vinyl. The bug-smeared windshield glares and it's hard for him to watch Joey walking away, waving once more over his shoulder, still carrying his broken piece of phone.

dutch
E L M

When I left Wisconsin, the disease was already toppling the heavy-crowned elms that for so long had made green tunnels of all our streets. But I didn't leave because the trees were dying, and I didn't go west because the disease hadn't yet crept that far. I'd simply reached the moving age, and as fast as I could, I sped past the elm stumps, then the endless stretches of the cornfields and dairy farms, and finally out into the plains. I wound up at the edge of the mountains, in Great Falls, surrounded by wheat, as far as my money would take me. I had no plans of ever turning around.

By the time I landed my first decent job I also had a wife, and though our first home was again shaded by rows of the giant trees, the slow death march of the elms couldn't have been further from my mind.

After a delay long enough to be frightening, our first child, Jeremy, was born, in the middle of a winter that broke all the records for cold. On business trips I'd hear of the temperatures in

Great Falls and have nightmares of boiler failure—returning home to find their two bodies curled by ice. That March the cold gave one last gasp and we read in the papers how the early calves froze to the ground in their placental sacks.

When that winter finally gave up, a pair of Great Falls park employees came down our street, stapling orange tags onto the first elms that would fall. I remembered back home in Madison they had painted black, tarry bands around the trunks of our elms, and feeling vaguely guilty, as if somehow I were the carrier of the disease, I asked the men about the tar, if they'd ever heard of it, if it wasn't something worth trying here.

They only shook their heads. "There's no stopping it," one of them told me. "Only hope is that some of them just somehow survive."

The next year they came back, felling the elms, grinding their stumps, replacing them with spindly little maples and locusts.

We never had another winter that hard, and Monica was pregnant again by the time the trees began to fall. Within six years Jeremy had two brothers and two sisters. After they came along, we sometimes called Jeremy the Ice Man, remembering those early years. He was always vaguely proud of the name, thinking the cold had been something he was tough enough to get through, whereas maybe his brothers and sisters wouldn't have been.

Though I traveled a lot, business was good and we moved to a bigger house in town. At night Monica and I stayed awake late, and I'd talk about trying something new, something without the travel. Monica wondered about finishing school because the kids wouldn't always be there, and maybe after they were gone she would be too old. We laughed at that, still young enough to laugh at the idea of being too old for anything.

It was all just daydreaming out loud. We had our house and our children, and our work went into them. This wasn't something we regretted or were bitter about. Not in the least. All our quiet talk in bed, after the kids were asleep, was our way of reaffirming this. We'd always fall asleep a little amazed at how lucky we were.

Driving home one spring, taking a new route that dropped down the bluffs to the Missouri, out of sight of the mountains and the horizon-to-horizon strips of wheat, I was surprised to find a narrow band of riverbank covered by a lone cornfield. That fast I was back home in Wisconsin, surrounded by brilliant green corn, the light hazier and heavier than it was out here in all the open.

After talking it over with Monica we bought the old farmhouse on that riverbank and began what we hoped would be a tradition of shutting down the Great Falls house after school and moving out to the country for the summers. Only then did we learn that the corn was just a lark; something the farmer wanted to try. "Too cold for it up here, really. Too short a season."

But that summer was hot and wet, perfect for corn, and the kids went wild: building dams in the tiny creek cutting to the big river; playing hide-and-seek in the cottonwoods. They caught frogs and turtles and grasshoppers, and ran laughing down the rows of corn when it was still only waist-high.

Our last day there that first summer, Monica and I made a game out of packing the station wagon, trying to make it fun because no one wanted to go home. When the kids got distracted or mopey I chased them, scaring them with sudden charges. They scattered and I'd scoop up one or the other, tickling them until they howled. Then I'd go back into the house for the next box. Once I let the kids knock me down, and they all dove in to tickle the monster man. We were red with laughing, and had bits of dead grass and leaves stuck to our hair and clothes.

Toward evening the car was loaded, and Tim, our youngest, was already asleep on the pile of bedding in back. As I started rounding up the rest of the tribe Jeremy gave one last run, wanting to be chased, and I started after him.

Jeremy surprised me, heading for the corn, which was ready for harvest and much taller than my head; something they'd avoided. But in he went, and so did I, having to slow and move sideways between the tight, towering stalks. The constant Great Falls wind rattled the stalks, and I laughed demonically, shouting, "I'm going to get you, Jeremy!" I barely heard him giggle and run, and I stepped through a row but the leaves cut my view short. I moved on, laughing and threatening, crossing rows now and then, unable to see or hear another thing.

I stood still, my ears straining against the childhood rustle of the plants, but Jeremy had lost me. Finally I shouted that he had won, that it was time to go. "Come on, Jeremy," I called, and headed back to where I thought the house was.

I didn't like the constant brushing of the corn against me; the slick whish of it in my ears. It stole my bearings. By the time I reached the edge where Monica and the rest of the kids were waiting, I half-expected to see Jeremy there taunting me, but the first thing Monica said was "Where's Jeremy?"

"He's hiding in there. He'll be out in a second," I said, but Monica's voice had a trace of the urgency I'd begun to feel thrashing through the last of the corn. She immediately started herding the rest of the kids to the car. I turned to the blank green wall, and shouted for Jeremy.

Back from the car, Monica said, "We'd better start looking."

"I can see why they didn't like playing in there," I said. "I'd forgotten what it was like."

"It's just corn," Monica said. "There's no place for him to go."

The car horn blared and I turned quickly but Monica touched my arm and said, "I told them to. Every minute. It'll give them something to do and it'll let Jeremy know which way to go."

"He's just hiding is all," I said, but I looked back up at the golden tassels waving in the wind, fringing the upper points of the wall. "Jeremy!" I shouted. "Enough is enough!"

"He's probably lost," Monica said. "Don't get mad."

"Well, I'll go back in," I said, hesitating. "You stay here in case he comes out."

"I'll go in too, over here."

I shrugged and ducked back into the green rows, knowing as soon as the flat, waxy leaves touched my face that we would have done better just waiting. This wasn't the wilderness after all, and he had to turn up soon.

I counted the rows I crossed so I could retrace my steps, and I shouted his name now and then. The car horn honked every minute, swirling in the wind, impossible to locate. Occasionally the horn gave quick, oddly timed bursts, and I pictured the bickering over who got to punch it next.

As I pushed more and more leaves away from my face it occurred to me that I had no idea how far this cornfield went on, how soon it dropped into the river. It had only been a field before, covered with corn instead of wheat, but otherwise just like every other field between here and town.

Crossing through yet another row I bumped into Monica and she gave a yelp of surprise that nearly brought tears to her eyes. I was startled too, my breath quicker than it had been an instant before. "We'll never find him in here," Monica said.

"Let's head back. That's probably him blowing the horn now. They're probably calling him the Corn Man already." I tried to sound reassuring, but I was hugging Monica in the middle of a jungle blackening with dusk, and our oldest child was missing.

We turned around, holding hands as we fought the corn. The sun set before we reached the house's clearing, but it was much lighter out of the smothering cover of the plants. For a moment things seemed more hopeful out in the open, but Monica's face was pale, her lips drawn tight and bloodless against her teeth. Her eyes flicked around the sides of the clearing, and she started for the car.

We stopped when we could see that Jeremy wasn't back.

Monica said she'd drive the dirt road that circled the corn. I'd run up the tractor track just this side of the little creek the kids had played in all summer. If Monica didn't see him on her first pass, she'd run to the farmer for help.

I gave Monica a hug before we split up and said, "Come on, Monica, it's only a cornfield. A tiny one. You should see them back home."

She smiled thinly, giving a shake of her head and a nervous giggle. "I know," she said. "We're being ridiculous."

But she turned for the car, and I ran to where the ruts of the tractor track cleaved the corn like a scar. We never said that he was anything but hiding in the corn, but we'd set up a search and started on it, even leaving the farmer to fall back on—to put our hope into if our initial sweep was a failure.

As I ran down the slash through the serried black-green ranks of the corn, I began to mumble, "It's just a cornfield," over and over. There were horrible pictures lurking at the edge of my mind that the chant held at bay. It was only a cornfield, something I'd played in as a kid. It wasn't a city, where anything bad could happen at any time. There was the river, though, and we were in the country, and I wondered if there were snakes out here, or bears. But I had never even thought of anything like that before, and I could still hear the occasional bleat of Monica's horn, not too far away on the other side of the field. It was only a cornfield, and nothing bad could really happen in something like that.

Then, before the search had even really started, I turned the slightest of bends in the path, one I didn't think could have hidden anything, and there was Jeremy, running in the wrong direction—

away from me—and when I called his name he ran even faster, as if it were me he was escaping. He looked over his shoulder when I called again, then turned and stopped. I ran in and scooped him off the ground. He was crying as hard as I'd ever seen him cry, the tears tracking down the sweaty dirt on his face. I rocked him back and forth, calling him the Ice Man, because he felt brave with that name, and I told him how scared I was, so his fear wouldn't embarrass him when it left.

He settled down a little before Monica drove into sight, bouncing wildly over the track that was never meant for any car. The lights caught us and I waved at her, to let her know we were all right, and I brushed at Jeremy's tears so the other kids wouldn't tease him.

Monica skidded to a stop, erupting from behind the wheel and pulling Jeremy away from me, crying already herself. She kissed Jeremy over and over, until he was crying again, too. Even some of the kids in the car were crying, seeing their mom so shaken, and I was trembling myself, all the bizarre flashes I had while running down this road without my son pouring back in on me. I wondered if the night would have been cold enough to kill him. I wondered if there might be old wells or sinkholes or something like that, that he could fall into and disappear. I even pictured him making it to some road I didn't know about, being picked up by somebody who would decide to keep him. That fast, I had imagined long nights holding Monica, going over every detail of watching Jeremy disappear forever into a row of corn that had no business growing in this country and would never be planted here again.

Putting my arms around both of them on the grassy road, I gently lifted them to their feet. I hugged Monica hard and took Jeremy from her arms, settling him onto my lap as I slipped behind the wheel, though he was far too big for that anymore. I held his hands on the steering wheel under my own hands, and said, "Why don't you drive us all on home, Ice Man?" Pretty soon the crying in the car fell behind us and Monica smiled at me and the kids started getting loud, fighting over their turns to drive, and though that was the most wonderful sound, I started to shake again, suddenly seeing all my children in those haunting poster black-and-whites, scattered vainly across the country.

We were on the highway then, flying past the short, safe wheat, the mountains hemming us in on the west, and I felt Jeremy's hands hot under mine. There was a scrape on his narrow, naked wrist, and I thought of him tripping in the desperate, ebbing light of the corn jungle, scraping himself on the brittle shards of last year's wheat. His sharp hipbones dug into me and I felt him try to turn the wheel, anticipating the next turn. I squeezed his hands a little tighter and gentled out the curve for him.

As I calmed, I stopped seeing the frightening pictures of missing children. Oddly enough, I thought of those men back home, when I was so young, painting the grim black rings around the still solid-looking trunks of our elms; trees that were already as good as dead. Those rings hadn't done a thing.

And, though I could see that clearly, I already knew that next year there would be rules about playing in the fields. Steering Jeremy's small, dirty hands through the next looping curve, I pictured Monica and myself as old people, holding each other in bed. In our big, quiet house we'll whisper, asking if we remember the evening the Ice Man was lost in the corn.

It will have become one of the family stories that gets told when the kids come home. They'll all laugh when I admit I was scared enough to picture bears eating my son in the cornfield. They'll laugh about the honking of the horn too, which most of them wouldn't have been old enough to really remember.

But holding Monica in the darkness, years and years from now, with our like thoughts of the towering corn and our separate

thoughts of our children spread out, facing all those dangers without us, I feel her breath quiet on my neck, and I still imagine I can
paint broad black bands around all of us.

lifesaving

Whenever somebody asks I always tell them, "It wasn't anything." Usually I'll add, "Anybody would've done the same," but who knows if that's true? They ask why I did it and I say, "I don't know," which is sure true enough.

At first I'd always look at the ground and smile a little, purposely trying to turn the ends of my smile down, like I was embarrassed and didn't really want to talk about it. That, of all of it, was the only thing I knew wasn't true. I didn't know why I did it and I didn't know if I'd ever do it again, and I didn't know if anybody else would have done it. But I sure knew I liked being looked up to and fussed over. That hadn't happened since my flirting days in the lifeguard chair. At first my only regret was that there hadn't been somebody videotaping, so I could've gotten on *Eye-Witness Video*, or *Rescue 911* even. But that's only how it was in the beginning.

Now I find out *911* might want to do it anyway. They called the other day when I was out, talked to Ellie, and I've told her to tell them I'm not home if they call again. I've got to figure things out before I talk to anybody like that.

The story, which you might already know, and you'd definitely know if there'd been anyone there with a video camera, wasn't anything much. I'd been fishing on the jetties off Galveston when this little pleasure boat chugs past. It stops right off from me, like they're trying to see if I've been catching anything. I wasn't. It's a second before I see the smoke and the guy lifting the engine hatch. Then boom, the boat goes up like a rocket. Gas leak, they say now.

It was almost dark and to tell the truth I wasn't fishing much. My line was out, sure, with a shrimp dragging my hook around, but mostly I was thinking how much I wanted to quit my job, but how I couldn't with Ellie and the kids. That went to wondering what it'd be like to leave them and go off somewhere new, maybe with Karen from the office. Then I started thinking about Karen and her cheerleader looks, wondering if she really was giving the signs I thought she might be, and what that would be like, and whether or not I'd miss Ellie, or the kids. Just daydreaming. Then the boat came around the jetty, like I said.

I sat up when the boat blew and for a little while I just sat and watched—watched the little pieces come back down, splashing into the water, the fire shooting up behind them, making the water all bright around the boat, like another sunset right in front of me. I never told anybody about waiting like that. Everybody thinks I jumped in the second the fireball went up, and that doesn't hurt anything.

To tell the truth I didn't get into the water until I heard the lady scream. "Rick!" is what she yelled, then, "Kevin!" Neither one answered. That's when I stopped thinking of what I was doing. Just stripped down and went.

I didn't see the gas burning on the water until after I'd swum out. It looked like a pretty small, little fire, and I dove under it. I'm not a bad swimmer, I mean I was a lifeguard back in high school, and I figured it wasn't anything. But I misjudged, or the wind shifted or something, and I came up in the middle of it. Complete accident. Just lucky for me I swim with my eyes closed. But that's where I lost my hair—burned off—and that's where I found the kid. Bumped into him already underwater as I dove back down and I just held on. When I came back up I was out of the flame and I held up what I'd found and saw it was this little boy, a little singed and already crying. I started for the jetty with him and as I was towing him in he surprised me, asking what my name was, as if we'd just met on the playground or someplace. I told him I was J.J. and I asked him what his name was and he told me, "Kevin."

Of course everybody talks about Kevin now. That was the big thing, swimming into the fire to get him, but like I said, I didn't even know he was there. Total accident.

But I hauled him back first and set him on the jetty next to my empty fish bucket. Then I went back for the lady. She wasn't screaming anymore and the fire was dying, which by then was my only light, so I breaststroked out, trying to see whatever I could. I must've swum up to twenty pieces of trash before I found her, treading water, quiet as a mouse. I talked to her, asked if she was all right, then wound up towing her in. She didn't say a word until she saw Kevin, when she kind of fell apart.

I went out one more time looking for Rick and was pretty close to giving up—I hadn't swum since high school and that'd been a while ago and I was worn right out—when I crossed paths with him. He was in a dead man's float, exactly like we'd used in our lifeguard classes, pretending we were dead and needing to be rescued. I flipped him over and started pulling him in but then wondered what that'd be like for that lady and kid. I tried picturing myself on the jetty, holding onto Amy, say, all burned, and having Ellie come out of the water dead.

It was completely dark by this time so I towed him up a little farther out on the jetty. I looked at him a minute and though I couldn't see much I stayed there until I was sure he was dead. I wedged him into the rocks and walked down to where I'd been fishing.

The lady and the kid were holding on to each other like glue, rocking back and forth, crying. I tried talking to them as I got dressed, though I wasn't sure if they heard a word or not. She kept her face pressed to his, petting his back, murmuring things I wasn't even sure were words, like Ellie will do, soothing Amy's skinned knees. Watching her hand going automatically back and forth below his shoulders I realized the kid was bald, and I wondered if I'd ever seen a bald kid before.

I tried getting dressed as fast as I could, but my pants clung to my wet legs and it took a long time to get them on. So I skipped my shirt and socks and just slipped on my shoes and trotted back to shore for the phone. They probably got the call taped for *911*.

I started back out to the two of them then, waiting for the sirens, and that's the first time I had any idea I got burned myself. My shoulders stung, like with a bad sunburn, and I reached up to them and I could feel something wrong with my skin. Then I noticed my head tingling, and I touched it and found out my hair was gone. I patted my head once and all of a sudden had to sit down.

I didn't get back up until the ambulances came. Even though my legs were pretty shaky I walked out the jetty with the rescue guys to show where the lady and the kid were. They kept trying to get me to sit down, telling me I was hurt, but I told them I was all right. I was a lifeguard and I needed to show them.

Once they got the kid and the lady loaded up I wandered up the jetty and pretended I'd just found the other guy, the man. They took him away too, but the lady didn't know about him until she was in the hospital, which I guessed was probably the best way to do it. Nobody knows that either—that I'd known about the man all along.

At the hospital they were wrapping me in bandages when the reporters found me. In the bright lights, with all of them asking everything at once, things got pretty confusing. I was still trying to figure out what I'd tell Ellie and pretty soon I was just nodding my head to whatever they said. That's how the waiting part got left out of the story, and the fact that I never meant to swim into the gas, never would have done it on purpose in a million years, that the whole Kevin thing was just an accident. They made up the story until I was doing the lifeguard swim straight through the fire as part of some big plan. And I agreed. Even Ellie doesn't know how it really went. That night I tried to tell her a little, but I was already just retelling the reporters' story.

After getting rid of the reporters Ellie settled down on my bed, me on my stomach because of my shoulders, and she started to cry all of a sudden. She crunched over and hugged me low around my waist and put her head into the small of my back. "How could you do that?" she wanted to know. "Why would you ever do that to us?"

That's when I first realized I didn't know why I'd do such a thing and that I'd probably never know. I wasn't even very sure I wanted to know. I felt bad about what I'd been daydreaming on the jetty, which were things I never planned on, but just the kind of things that pop into your head, like when you're driving and see a huge semi coming at you and you wonder, Why not just swerve into him? When you wonder why you don't do that—what difference would it make?—you're not really planning anything, you're just wondering what it is that keeps you from it. Kind of seeing what's worthwhile. Not nearly as bad as it sounds.

But with Ellie's tears in my back it sounded pretty awful and when I went back to work, where they had banners about the hero all over the place, and my boss came over and told me they'd take care of all my medical costs—which weren't much, all the burns being quick kinds of things, nothing worse than second degree, and not much of that—I spent most of my time trying to avoid Karen, because of what I'd been thinking about on the jetty that night.

They took me out for drinks to celebrate my return, but after one round I told them I still had to take it pretty easy. With all of them telling the stories they'd heard on the news, I just wanted to be home with Ellie, who never talked about it, though she once told me of course she was proud of me, but mostly she was just all of a sudden scared to death for our family. Like I was going to swim through burning gasoline every time I walked out the door.

So I left, but not before Karen cornered me by the front door, telling me she knew from the first that there was something about me, something that would make me do daredevil things. Out in my car I smiled again, knowing the signs I'd thought I'd seen in Karen were real. It'd been a long, long time since I'd had that kind of dangerous, wanted feeling—like all of a sudden a whole new world's opening up, one that's going to fill in all the corners of my dreams—and even as I pulled out of the lot I wished there was some way I could go back into the bar. But I'd already made up my excuse to get out and I had to stick to it.

Back home Ellie had dinner ready and we sat down to it all together, Ellie, Amy, Kyle, and me. Used to be we'd eat around the TV, Ellie feeding Kyle in her lap, but ever since the accident Ellie made us eat together, "Like a family," she'd say. I liked it.

Ellie asked how the party had gone and I said something about being tired about always talking about the accident, and hearing about it.

She smiled at me then, putting a tiny slice of meat in Kyle's mouth. "I'm glad to hear that. It's gotten so it's like neither one of us ever did anything else in our lives. Like we don't even have our own lives anymore."

I nodded, the warm idea of Karen's come-on signs making it hard for me to concentrate on simple dinner talk.

"The mayor called while you were at your party," Ellie said suddenly. "They want to give you some award. Have a big, huge party for you."

I glanced up at her. "I think we could pass on that," I said.

"Me too," Ellie said, laughing a little in relief. "Me too. Can you imagine what it will be like to just get back to our own lives again?"

I wasn't sure I could imagine that, but I said, "Wouldn't that be nice?"

Most everybody'd I'd ever so much as passed in the street, plus a whole pile of total strangers, came to the country club dinner where the mayor gave me the Metcalf Award. I was all healed up by then, not even any scars, though the new skin on my shoulders was still pretty pink. But I still liked all the attention then, and I'd been having my hair cut super short, eighth inch, as if it had just been burned off.

Ellie said it looked good, but I knew she didn't like it. Ever since we were married she's always kind of absentmindedly messed with my hair, just walking by and taking the trouble to touch me, pet my hair smooth. She said the new short stuff tickled her hand.

But at the banquet it was short, and I knew I looked tough. Like somebody who'd swim through fire without a thought.

While the mayor talked I looked out at the crowd, not wanting to hear the made-up stories one more time. I picked Karen out right away, not sitting at the table with everyone else from work, but at her own table, with three other women who looked just like her, lean and hard, like the people you always see playing beach volleyball when you have to go to work.

Ellie was sitting next to me at the main table, with Kyle in her lap dressed to the nines in a blue blazer I'd never seen before. Amy was next to her, so excited she'd nearly wet her pants.

Since having Kyle, though it's been almost two years now, Ellie's been having trouble getting back her shape, and when Karen smiled at me, having caught my eye that fast, I pictured her running across the sand away from a volleyball net, muscles strung out tight, while I rise up out of the black water carrying Kevin and his mom.

They were there too, Kevin and his mom, on the other side of the podium. I hadn't seen them since they'd left the hospital. The fire had just reached Kevin and hadn't burned him any worse than me. I noticed his hair, which was blond, had already grown out a few inches and I felt a little embarrassed about my bullet head. His mom hadn't been hurt at all, but was in the hospital the whole time Kevin was. She smiled at me when she saw me but her eyes were dark, like holes, like she'd walked into a door or something, and I wondered if something had happened to her I hadn't heard about. When she got up to speak the whole place went dead silent.

I stared at my napkin when she said how, though her life had been shattered, a total stranger had risked his own just to give her back enough pieces to try and put hers together again.

That wasn't true at all. I hadn't risked my life for anything like that. I hadn't even guessed I'd risked my life. I still never thought of it like that. But staring at the folds of my napkin and listening to her I realized I hadn't ever thought much about her. Just of me. While I was making eyes at Karen this lady was wondering what to do with the pieces of her life.

She had to stop speaking for a moment and no one so much as cleared their throat. Finally she said, "You go out for a little bit of fun, a boat ride, and, and you just can't expect things to turn so awful. And you can never expect anyone to do something like Mr. Nahlen did for me. You can just never expect to be rescued like that." She touched me then on the shoulder and I nearly hopped out of my skin. She gazed at me through her dark cave-eyes, and she whispered, "Thank you so much for bringing Kevin back." Then she hugged me and I had to get out of my chair to hug her back and over her shoulder all I could see was Karen, her eyes bright as knife points, smiling at the daredevilry she saw in me.

Then we sat back down so the mayor could give me the plaque and Ellie squeezed my leg so hard I thought something was wrong. I leaned her way and she whispered, "I'm sorry about everything I said. I'd only seen losing you. I hadn't thought what you did for her." She had tears in her eyes, and looking out at the crowd I saw she wasn't the only one. I thought maybe that's all that made Karen's so startlingly bright.

The country club was where I'd worked as a lifeguard in high school, the only time I'd ever set foot in the place, but they made a big deal out of that and when the dinner was over they said they'd open up the bar. That nearly caused a stampede and Ellie looked at me hopelessly then gave me a quick hug, saying, "I'll take the kids home." Then she hugged tighter, tapping my back with the plaque she was taking home for me, and said, "Go easy, J.J." She let go of me to run her hand over my bristles and said, "Call if you can't find a ride."

I waved my arm around the room, as if it'd be hard finding a ride, and said, "I'll be fine. I'm going to duck out of here first chance I get. Place gives me the creeps."

We both smiled and then the mayor took me by the elbow and Ellie was gone and I didn't duck out at the first chance. Or the second.

I found a ride that night, or she found me maybe. Karen wasn't drinking, just soda water with slices of lemon. I'd had more drinks put into my hands than I did the day I turned twenty-one. When the party finally broke she was standing right next to me, saying, "Why don't I give you a lift?"

In her car she chatted about what a nice party it had been, but I was crashing fast. It was drizzling, the wipers on intermittent, and I stared at them, trying to guess exactly when they'd make their next move. She asked, "Really, J.J., what made you do it?"

I said, "Do what?" and her laugh tinkled through the car, sounding nice. She put her hand over mine and said, "Don't be so modest."

"I don't know why I did it at all," I said. "Anybody would've. I just happened to be there." I was so good at that answer by then I could run it off even with her hand where it was.

"Well I don't think anybody would have done it," she said, easing on the brakes for the watery shimmer of a red light. When the car stopped she leaned over and whispered, "I'm so proud of you," and she kissed me hard, on the mouth, and I kissed back, though I wondered how she could be proud of me. She didn't even know me.

It was late and there wasn't any traffic and we stayed at that light through a few changes, long enough for me to find out she was just as hard under her blouse as she looked, which somehow only made me think of Ellie, how she used to be that way too. I broke off our grappling, and there we sat at a red light, the wipers going on and off, the windshield a little foggy on the inside. Karen moved her blouse around so it fit again but didn't bother closing the top few buttons that had worked open. I hit the defrost to high so I couldn't hear the secret rustlings of her clothes, and hoped for the light to change.

"Well," she said, letting out a lot of breath.

I looked at the light, at the tiny points of rain collecting on the glass before the wiper came along again.

"Where should we—" she started, but I cut her off by saying, "I better get home."

"J.J.," she said, laughing a little, and I said "I better get home" again before she could finish whatever she was going to suggest.

The light turned green and she edged forward. "You've started a fire here, J.J. Aren't you going to help me put it out?"

"I'm done with fires," I said, rubbing my own prickly scalp. She caught me doing that and laughed again, her laugh more nervous than before, and she reached out to rub my hair too. I couldn't help flinching.

"Easy," she whispered. "Time for you to rescue me, hero. Save me from my burning building."

"Time for me to be getting home," I said, though not as surely as before. I was thinking of all that stiff lace over her breasts. Ellie sometimes still wore her nursing bras if they happened to be what she found in the drawer in the morning. I was thinking how nice it would be to undress her, to release all that myself, the quick slip of buttons through silk holes, instead of lying in bed while Ellie stripped down after her last check on the kids, leaving her clothes in a rumple at the side of the bed.

Karen was driving again, going straight forward instead of any direction that would take us somewhere in particular. I reached over to slip another button free, but stopped with my hand in the air, thinking of the hot, crinkly feel of the skin on my shoulders, when things on the jetty had finally slowed enough for me to think.

Karen took one hand off the wheel and plucked mine out of the air. She placed my hand on her, inside her shirt, whispering something I didn't catch. But I couldn't close my hand, couldn't make it do anything soft or teasing. I closed my eyes and thought that if I dove right now my arms would wrap around Kevin again, and I would surface in a moment in a quiet, dark place out of the flames, both of us singed, though I, at least, wouldn't know it for a while yet.

I pulled my hand back and set it in my lap. "I can't do this," I said. "I can't do this to Ellie."

"Ellie's not here," Karen said, her voice more nervous than ever. Her hand followed mine to my lap and I let it stay there longer than I should have. Then I moved it carefully away.

"J.J.," Karen said, sounding exasperated. She pulled off the road next to the park. The wipers kept up their disjointed sweeps. "J.J.," Karen said again when I looked away from the sparkling points of her eyes. "Whatever happened to my man who swam through an ocean full of burning gasoline?"

"That never happened," I said. "It was all an accident. I didn't even know Kevin was there."

Karen touched me again, saying, "Modesty," but I turned her hand away and said, "Really, that's how it happened, and I wouldn't do it again, for anything. She's a total stranger."

I couldn't stop thinking of the lump of Ellie's clothes beside the bed. "I got to go home now."

Karen didn't say anything for a long time. When she did speak all she said was, "I don't think I'll drive you home to your wife."

I didn't answer and she said, "That's not what I want. And I don't think that's what you really want."

She made one more move for me and I was out of the car before I quite realized I'd grabbed the door handle. "I'm sorry, Karen. I can't do this again."

"Ah," Karen said, leaning over to look me in the eye. "Again? Who was she? From the office? Once bitten twice shy?" She tried laughing again. "Get in the car, J.J."

I stared at her, lit badly by the dome light, her blouse falling open, exposing just the start of what I was diving away from. "That's not what I mean. Not like that."

"What do you mean then?" she asked.

She kept staring at me and I blurted, "I found that lady's husband, all drowned and dead and I dragged him away so she wouldn't see what had happened to her. I can't let that happen to Ellie."

Karen sat up then and I suddenly felt so safely at home I told her I'd see her on Monday and thanks for the ride. She said, "You won't see me like this on Monday, J.J.," raising her voice so I could hear after I closed the door. "Last chance," she shouted, and I turned, expecting to see my house before me, having forgotten that Karen hadn't actually driven me home.

I was trying to pierce the gloom, wondering what had happened to our house, my back still to the car when Karen pulled out fast, screeching the tires for an instant. I watched her red lights fade into the drizzle and I turned back to look again at the dark, empty space where I'd thought my home was. Then I began to walk, the drink and everything else collapsing inside of me, making the trip last forever.

The rain soaked through my suit before I reached my front door and I fumbled in my pockets for my keys. The bedside light was on in our room, spilling into the hallway. I hadn't expected Ellie to wait up for me and I had a guilty second wondering what she knew. I wasn't sure if I could face her right away so I went into the kitchen and drank a lot of water, hoping it would offset the booze in the morning. Then I sat on the tub edge and undressed, throwing my clothes over the shower curtain to dry.

I walked naked into the bedroom but Ellie wasn't waiting up for me. The light was on and her back was to it. I flicked off the light and listened to her quiet, relaxed breathing and I crawled in with her, my cold front to her warm back. In her sleep she wriggled away from my chill but I held her with my arms so she couldn't get away.

Under my hands I felt what I wished was all the hardness and laciness I could ever want, but I still thought of Karen anyway, wondering if I'd missed something I should've had, regardless of the risks. Even as I pictured Kevin's mom at home in her bed alone; alone for a long, long time without wanting to be, I wished I'd stayed with Karen a little longer. It seemed like I'd given up something maybe I'd earned by swimming into that fire. In the next few days I could be starring in *911*, who knows, and here I was, the same J.J. I'd always been.

Thinking like that was the same as thinking about swerving into a semi, though, and in the darkness of our room I began to realize what it was that always kept me from doing the stupid things I thought about. I decided right then that I'd grow my hair back, putting the flames behind me. I clutched Ellie tighter, though she'd warmed me enough she didn't squirm away anymore. Then I closed my eyes to slip safely and quietly below the gasoline, as if, in a way, it was still just a stranger I held in my arms.

play
BALL

The Cubbies were everybody's dream, of course. White Sox in a pinch. I mean, you could at least see yourself in the pinstripes with that old lettering and think that'd be all right, till you can swap leagues and really be a true Cub, one of the guys you've spent your entire life watching. Imagine.

But getting drafted went way past dreams. Still in high school. By the Dodgers. Not the Cubs, but still way hotter than anything ever—even my shutout in the city championships. The Dodgers have been around. I mean it wasn't like I got wasted on the Marlins or the Rockies. And I'd still get back home. Playing *against* the Cubs would be almost as big.

Party? Man oh man, did we party. Next day, head pounding, I went out and had LA cut into the sides of my crew cut. One on each temple.

Even so, I've been around. It's not like I thought I'd start the home opener in L.A. or anything.

But, for crying out loud, rookie-league ball? Stepping off the plane in Great Falls? Rookie league. In Montana! Not even single-A ball! Took a taxi out to the park. Middle of the night. Hungover.

I dodged through the golf course sprinklers beyond the outfield wall and climbed over, the same way I did in Chicago before the last city game, just to get in there for the feel of the place. Landed hard on the warning track. In the moonlight I could make out the ads covering the wooden wall. City Chevrolet, A. T. Klemens Plumbing and Heating. I wondered how many contracts A. T. Klemens got from the hicks who came to watch the Great Falls Dodgers.

I walked over the whole field in the darkness. I'd played on better in high school. But finally I stood on the mound and closed my eyes. The rubber wasn't in, but even so I could nearly bring up the opening-day roar of Wrigley. I slept in the dugout, freezing, letter jacket wrapped around me.

First thing, first team meeting, some guy comes up and touches the LA on the side of my head—slaps, more like it. "Ain't little league no more," he says. "Grow up."

Come to find out he was up here last year too. Two years with the Great Falls Dodgers. No wonder. Dead-end ride to nowhere. I let my hair grow out, though. Sure as hell wasn't going to cut GF up there. GF. That's what it said on our caps, looking just like L.A.'s caps, only somebody got the letters wrong. Way wrong.

You wouldn't believe the season if I told you. Bus rides. Not bus rides to the airport. Bus rides clear to Canada. Hours and hours in the diesel. Only to play in places like Lethbridge, against the Mounties. Can you believe it? Or Medicine Hat. What the hell? Medicine Hat! Where did these places come from? We've had games called due to wind. Wind!

First day in they decide I'm a first baseman. "No way!" I say, "I'm a pitcher."

"You're whatever we say you are. Got that, L.A.?" the coach says back. Already they're all calling me L.A.

"Check the reports," I say. "Lowest ERA ever in the history of Chicago. Shut them down in the last game of—"

"Hey, everybody," the coach calls out. "Any of you want to sit down and listen up? L.A.'s gonna tell us about his high school career again."

A chorus of "Shove it"s and "Save it"s and, "Grow up already"s.

It's not like I expected too much. I know minor league ball. I know it's a springboard to the bigs. But this was way less than anybody should have to put up with. I mean, my last year in high school I had the lowest ERA in the city. Chicago's a big place.

From the mound here you can see golf carts cruising the city course, where any gopher ball would land, then a little hump of hills, and beyond that not a single thing between me and Chicago. Nothing but nothing for a thousand miles.

The season runs half of June, all July, and August, and the first week of September. Six days off the whole time. None of them back-to-back. Busing and sandlot about all it is. Packed into the bus with a bunch of rubes from Oklahoma and Kentucky, even a guy from Australia, all thinking they're on the express to the bigs. Pathetic.

But by the end of July the only real pitcher they have is yanked to San Antonio, for double-A ball, and I finally get the nod. On the mound throwing B.P. I'm rusty but it feels good and I start pitching. Coach yells for me to throw. "This ain't the Series," he shouts.

Though I hate to say it, the first action I get is in relief. Me, a born-and-bred starter. Men at the corners, nobody out and we're already down by two. "Thanks a heap," I say out loud to myself.

And the fans. Like Gomez going to San Antonio was some plot I hatched up on my own. Closest they had to the bigs was Seattle, or Colorado now, if you count the losingest record in baseball as the bigs. In high school people would come just to watch me pitch.

I stayed a reliever, pitching until the fielding broke down, a few innings usually, then getting booed off the mound for six unearned runs. *Unearned* and they're booing like I walked in the final run of the Series. Tries my patience and I wind up suspended for three games for flipping the crowd the bird. Wasn't any peace after that. Week-long road trip right after, but they got memories like elephants.

Up in Medicine Hat I faced a guy named Willie Powell. Big boy, weak on sliders, but he could hit. Here he is playing for the Medicine Hat Blue Jays, but they all call him Boog. As in Boog Powell. Start chanting it every time he comes to the plate— *Boooooog!* It doesn't get much more pathetic than that. I shut him down with a slider on a three-two that leaves him standing with his teeth in his mouth. At least he plays first base, same as the real Boog, though I wouldn't swear the fans know that.

I finally get a start. In Great Falls, which I figure the coach set up on purpose. Fans went nuts, throwing garbage onto the field until the PA man has to warn them to stop. Standing on the mound, trying to get my last warm-ups in, get my head into the game, and I have to put up with that. I mean, standing there with a great big GF on my cap.

The coach trots out to the mound before the first batter gets up. Fans go wild again, thinking I'm getting pulled before I've thrown a pitch. I don't even want to look at him. Just turn his way and wait.

But the coach is a different guy. "Take it easy now kid," he says to me. "We want to get a look. This isn't the Series. Forget the crowd. It's just a game."

"In Great Falls," I answer him, but he lets it slide right off.

"Just throw your stuff. Don't tighten up and don't try to kill anybody. Pretend you're back in high school." He can't help a little smile then and as he walks off I think, "My high school career would be the highlight of your whole life."

But I'm shook, I guess. Walk the first guy on five pitches. I never walk people. Pinpoint control. It's been a long time since I started. I tell myself that, slap myself in the face with my glove, tell myself to bear down. Crowd going wild, but they go nearly silent in my head, and I smile, knowing I can do anything if I can do that.

Next two batters on six pitches. Don't even touch it. Not even a foul back.

Boog comes in at cleanup. In my mind there's nobody on first, just this big galoot at the plate, weak on sliders. I wave off the catcher's sign, which comes from the dugout, and wait until I get a slider.

I set and as soon as it leaves my hand I know it's perfect and I'm going to get him on three straight sliders.

Boog hits it over the fence, over the billboard Marlboro Man's right shoulder. As he rounds second, his home-run trot a thing of practiced beauty, Boog points at me and then at his head, letting me know he won the thinking game that time. I try to remember what I threw him in Medicine Hat, but for the first time ever I can't recall the exact sequence. Sliders, I figure.

We get a few back in the third, but I give up a few more. All I can see is the Marlboro Man, big hick guy you might run into just outside this park in Great Falls, Montana. He's a long way from home, three hundred and eighty feet, easy. I got my nose rubbed in it that time. Ball lying out there on the fairway, carts detouring around it, wondering how the hell it got clear out there. Maybe some kid's already snagged it, hoarding a souvenir of Boog's early days, thinking it'll be a gold mine when Boog's ripping up the bigs.

Boog doubles his second time up, but I strand him there.

By the sixth I know I'm around a hundred pitches, facing the hook. We're only down by one and I've settled in, cooling the last five straight, but one hundred is the limit. Great coaching. By the numbers. I had four straight complete games in high school. Unheard-of.

When Boog comes up for the third time the crowd begins to leak into my head. I take off my cap and wipe the sweat away. It's another scorcher in Great Falls. Crowd is going so nuts. "Boog, Boog, *Booooooog*!" Whose side are they on? I know I got to put them away, but then their chanting gives way to a roar and out of the corner of my eye I see the coach come out of the dugout. I go limp as a rag, waiting.

All he says is, "You want another crack at him?"

I nod and he slaps my rear and walks away. Can't tell if the crowd is booing or yelling for Boog.

My concentration is blown away. I can see Boog, I can hear the crowd. That should never happen. I'm wondering what I should use. Suddenly I can't even remember what the second pitch was. The one he doubled off me.

I step off the rubber and wipe away more sweat. Crowd gears up all over. "Go with the sign," I whisper to myself. I take a big breath, step up to the rubber. I get the sign. I nod, then look down at my shoes, putting everything away where it belongs.

I smile and lift my arms to my chest, only looking to the plate as I begin to raise my leg.

Boog's not even in the box. I throw the pitch anyway, a crippled duck, just to avoid the balk. But there wasn't any chance of that, I realize. Time was out. He wasn't in the box.

What he was was laughing. He stood just outside the box laughing, teeth white in his black face. Then he shook his head and touched his bat to his temple. Some kind of salute. Crowd can't go any wilder.

Behind the rubber I realize Boog is living it. The out-of-town crowd loving him up. Two for two against me already. Boog's hamming me bad, and in his head I know he isn't wearing a Medicine Hat uniform. He's in Toronto, keeping the world championship in Canada year after year. Single-handedly.

You miserable jerk, I think. Wake up. You're playing for Medicine Hat, Alberta, Canada. You're a million miles from Toronto. A million miles from anywhere. But when I look up, already into my windup, he's standing ready, still smiling. All I see is his teeth, how he's in game seven of his own personal world series and how he doesn't even imagine that he won't blow this ball clean through the Marlboro Man so they'll remember him forever. Boog, Boog, *Booooooog*!

I uncork straight heat. A fastball as hard as I've ever thrown. Straight at his pathetic grin.

But Boog is quick, a true athlete, and even before the catcher starts up out of his crouch, he's falling away, ducking his head. The pitch catches him straight on top of the helmet, which really I'm glad for.

His legs start to go, but he catches himself, his helmet knocked clear, and he looks at me for an instant, still smiling. Then he comes.

The catcher and the umpire tangle up trying to stop him, not even laying a hand on him. He's coming full-sprint, still carrying his bat, and I plant my right foot back to take him. Throw my mitt aside.

He lifts the bat just before he gets there. I see everything, the dugouts streaming out, my big first baseman charging in fast but too late. I raise my glove arm to take the swing of the bat, but Boog goes down under the flying block of my shortstop. Same guy who'd slapped me in the head my first day in Great Falls. Who'd told me I wasn't in high school anymore. Even faster than Boog.

I got blindsided myself then. Somebody from the dugout. I went down, but everybody was there then, no room for punches or damage, just a roll on the grass, a pile of bodies. I lay under the squirming weight, the lowest earned run average in the history of Chicago high schools, somebody pulling at my hair, which was too short to get a grip on, though the LAs on my temples were long gone.

For the first time all game I couldn't tell you what was going on in the crowd. Only thing I knew for sure, Boog never once stopped smiling. Boog was on his way to the bigs.

the baby-
SITTER

Bill's parents were on the road. They'd be pulling up the drive anytime, today probably, though maybe he still had until to-morrow. His wife, Sarah, had been missing for three days but Bill still had no idea what he would tell his parents. He guessed he would wing it—see what came out of his mouth and take it from there. He figured he'd get through the hug and the handshake, if he could control the trembling. Then his mother would tell him how nice the house looked and she would glance around an extra time. She would ask where Sarah was.

She'd be the one to toss it right out in the open like that, but Bill was more worried about his father, who, after reaching out for the handshake, would fall back behind Bill's mother and stand quietly, looking around the small house much more slowly than she had with her darting glances.

His father would see what was missing, what no one could see with flashing glimpses no deeper than the surface of things. All the things were still there: the long-dried corsage stuck in the neck of an empty, expensive champagne bottle, her dusty textbooks lined into the bookcase, even the bookcase—planks and cinder blocks. When he'd cleaned in preparation for their arrival, Bill had left a pair of her running shoes beside the couch where she'd last taken them off. But he knew his father would see how none of this was the same anymore, how her absence had taken almost everything that had ever been in the room.

When he heard the car slow out on the street, Bill jumped up, unable to keep his heart from racing. It was his parents though, not Sarah, or the police, and he watched the truck turn into the driveway, humping over the rise of the culvert. He looked around his little living room and before moving toward the door he kicked Sarah's running shoes under the couch. The couch's skirt dropped back behind them, as if the shoes had never been there at all.

His parents rang the bell and Bill was there to meet them and everything went as Bill had known it would. He was looking at his father when his mother asked where Sarah was. Already his father would not look him in the eye. When his mother asked the question a second time, his father looked at the books. He studied them a long time and Bill wondered if he was looking for new titles, or checking for marks in the dust, seeing which books had drawn any interest in the past.

Bill thought, for just an instant, how nice it would have been to see them just a few days ago, how he always liked to see them. He said, "She's house-sitting for one of the doctors. Baby-sitting, really." She had done that once, but Bill was surprised to hear such an odd story come out. He was still panicky and in the instant he spoke he felt that if he could keep his parents from knowing about Sarah maybe they could make him feel as safe as they always had. Baby-sitting would not be an easy story to follow through, but it was out now and Bill would make the best of it.

"She can get away for dinner, though," his mother said, barely making it a question.

"She's baby-sitting, Mom. With children. She has to stay with them."

Bill felt his father glance at him and he took his mother's coat, shaking the misty little rain from it before putting it in the closet. His father was looking at other things when he handed his coat over and Bill shook it too.

"Come in," Bill said. "You don't have to stand in the door."

They dropped down the steps to the living room, which seemed to ring with emptiness. His mother said, "Well, call her and have her bring the kids along. How many are there?"

"Three. And you don't want to have dinner with a bunch of kids. Maybe she can sneak over for a lunch before you go."

"I don't mind kids. It'll be fun."

"Dad will be wild to have those ruggers tearing around the table. I know that." Bill looked straight at his father then, for help.

His father nodded. "I'm worn-out. Something quick and easy sounds good to me. We'll have plenty of time to see Sarah."

They worked that over for a while and Bill showed them to their room, which was his room, his and Sarah's. "I'll sleep on the foldout, Mom. Nothing else would make sense. You can't sleep in the camper in my own driveway. The couch will be fine. There's two of you. You get the bed."

His father agreed with that too, and Bill left them to settle in. He walked into his empty living room and took several deep breaths. He'd never lied much and he was surprised how easy it had been. He wondered what he could have done with that knowledge if he'd had it in time. He almost smiled, thinking how he could have had affairs, how easily they could have been hidden from Sarah. But he didn't smile. Instead the shaking returned, and the gnawing in his stomach, as if he hadn't eaten for days. He never would have had an affair, and he certainly couldn't have lied to Sarah that easily. But his mind had taken to wondering about all sorts of things he might have done, good and bad. The pictures materialized at the slightest wisp of thought, before he had a chance to alter or enhance them.

Bill's parents came down the hallway and Bill pushed his trembling hands into his pockets. For an instant, seeing their familiar faces, he nearly blurted, We had a fight and Sarah's gone and I don't know where and I don't know if she's coming back. But he simply opened the door and said he would drive. In the rain again, his mother asked if he didn't need a coat and Bill said, "No, I'll be all right."

The dinner was quick and easy and Bill managed to talk about his work. The summer had gone well, he said, the timing working out nicely. He'd been busy painting houses all summer and now that the weather was turning cold it looked as if he'd be able to paint interiors straight through to spring. Sarah's receptionist job was as secure as could be. The doctors in the office were all old and their practice had been well established decades ago.

But the doctors were all richer than a housepainter would ever be, he said, even managing a laugh. The one Sarah was baby-sitting for was off to Bermuda or Bimini or someplace like that. He usually stayed a month, Bill added, so there was no hope Sarah would be back before they left. Sometimes he even called and asked if it would be all right with Sarah if he stayed a little longer. He paid Sarah to stay in the house, so it was always all right.

Bill's mother said it was awfully inconsiderate of an educated man to ask newlyweds to be apart for that long a time. .

"We're not newlyweds, Mom. We've been married over a year now."

"You're newlyweds until the first crisis. We were newlyweds until we tried to have children."

Bill crumpled his napkin and put it on the table. He knew they'd planned a large family, and he knew he'd been born a decade after they'd given up hope. "We're not newlyweds, Mom," he said, and he was that close to telling her. Instead he said, "Besides, I can stay over there anytime I want. He always asks if we'll both move in. He says it'd make him feel safer, about the house and the kids."

"Well, why don't you, then?"

"We've got our own house, Mom. Who's going to make me feel safe?"

Bill marveled at how well he was doing this. Even the nervous quaver in his voice had not lasted long. But he did wonder about that—about who was going to make him feel safe, and he lost the thread of the conversation. His father caught him off guard when he asked how old the kids were.

"Teenagers," Bill said. "They just need someone there to see what time they get in at night." He looked at his mother. "You know what a problem that can be."

"Oh, you gave me such fits," his mother said, laughing. "I could never sleep until you were in the house."

Bill laughed about it too, admitting some things about the times he used to get home, but he felt his father's gaze. He was thinking, Bill guessed, that no one would expect teenagers to run around a restaurant table. No one called them ruggers either.

His parents went to bed as soon as they got in that night. They'd been in Montana that morning, and had driven nearly four hundred miles, a good one hundred miles farther than was their practice. Customs had been a nightmare, they said. They had no idea what the Canadians thought two retired people would be smuggling in, but they had made them unpack the entire camper. They asked Bill what they were looking for and Bill said he didn't know, he really hadn't been a Canadian that long.

They laughed at that, and his mother said he was as much a Canadian as they were. Bill stepped to the door and said good night.

His father tapped him on the shoulder once, and said it was good to see him again. That was not at all something he usually did and Bill knew he'd made a mistake about the kids' age. He said, "Good to see you guys, too. Good night." He closed their door behind him.

Bill turned off the lights in the living room and moved into the kitchen. After closing the door he turned on the light. He sat down at the Formica table and picked at the ribbed chrome edging. He wished there was a light in the room that was not so glaring.

But he did not want to be caught sitting in the dark so he left the light on and pulled the morning paper closer to his side of the table. If anyone came in he could pretend he was reading. Then Bill sat back and closed his eyes against the brightness.

He thought of the window across the room and how, on a clear day, the mountains stood in it, shimmery and blue, not all that real looking. When he had married Sarah he'd looked forward to moving to a different country, even if it was only Canada, and living in the mountains. He'd been to Calgary with her before, but somehow he'd forgotten that Calgary was out in the endless flats, fifty miles from any mountains. Provo, where he'd grown up, and where his parents still lived, was much closer to the peaks.

He wondered where in the world Sarah was now and he resurrected a prayer he hadn't used in years, hoping she was all right.

Bill heard a door creak and he opened his eyes and hunched over his paper. No sound followed though and soon he was staring at his fingers. He pulled out his pocketknife and scraped at a thick drop of paint on his thumbnail. He peeled it off, nicking the nail slightly with the sharp blade. He was wiping the paint off the blade when his father edged through the kitchen door.

He looked rickety in the loose pajamas, his thin hair already mussed from the pillow. He smiled at Bill and Bill held out the knife with the paint on it. "Stuff gets everywhere," he said.

"I'd've thought you'd have gone to bed too. Working tomorrow?"

"I took a day, since you were up."

His father nodded. "I'm too tired to sleep. I usually have a little whiskey when that happens."

"Cupboard behind you," Bill said, and his father found the still-full bottle of whiskey he'd left when they were up for the wedding. "Glasses are one over."

His father sat across from Bill at the table and poured himself a light inch of whiskey. Bill shook his head when his father held the bottle to him. He watched his father take his first sip and said, "What the hell," and got himself a glass too. He sat back, rocking the chair on its back legs, and took a sip small enough he wouldn't wince.

"We're going to try to go up to Jasper," his father said.

"It's pretty there. They'll have snow with this rain, but it shouldn't be too bad this early. You'll like it."

They both sipped their drinks and didn't say anything else.

Bill looked around the small kitchen. "Are you going to cross over the mountains then, from Jasper?"

His father brushed some whiskey away from his lip and nodded.

"Go back down through Idaho?"

"No. I think we'll go all the way over to Vancouver. Mom wants to see the gardens. Then through Seattle and Portland. We may even go into California and swing through Tahoe on the way back."

"Sounds good."

"We went too far today though."

"You can stay and rest up tomorrow."

His father said that sounded good then fell back into silence. He ran his finger around the edge of his glass, circling and circling. "You two still so crazy about each other? You and Sarah?"

It wasn't the kind of question his father asked and Bill grinned in surprise. Then he wasn't sure he could hold even a smile and he nodded his head and hid his mouth behind his glass.

His father nodded again. "You like it up here? In Canada?"

"Sure. It's pretty enough."

"Utah isn't so hard on the eyes."

"There's a lot of work here."

"Provo too."

"Sarah's from here, Dad. We knew this is where we'd live."

"Her parents aren't alive."

"She likes it here, Dad."

"I think it'd be odd—being a foreigner." His father screwed the cap onto the bottle and set his glass down over its neck. "Pretty poor pickings for Mormons, aren't we?"

"We're all right, Dad."

They both looked at the bottle and Bill smiled at the things his father could think about. A bottle of whiskey with a single inch out of it in a year.

"You wouldn't believe how time can hang," his father said suddenly. He stood up and put the bottle back in the cupboard. He stretched and yawned. "Seems like we've been traveling since I retired. If it wasn't for your mother I think I'd try to get my job back."

Bill did know how time could hang but he didn't say anything and his father moved to the doorway. "You and Sarah talk about having kids yet?"

Bill looked at the table. "Some. You know." He heard his father stop at the door. "We'll see."

His father pushed open the door. "'Some, you know, we'll see.'" He twisted the doorknob in his hand, and Bill listened to it rattle. "Don't wait too long. You don't have forever. It might take as long as it did for your mother and me."

His father said good night without waiting for Bill to answer. Bill watched the empty door in the bright light after he had gone. Tomorrow would be Sarah's fourth day and nothing was any easier than it had been the first hour after the police had left. His stomach was still twisted with fear and Bill was sure he hadn't done a thing right since she'd disappeared. He didn't think he was right hiding it from his parents, but he couldn't have it out in the open, under this garish light, where it would be the only possible subject for conversation.

Bill's fingers trembled as he set his glass on the counter and he stared at his hand as if it were something new in the house. He looked again at the empty door where his father had stood, with his chest visibly sagged under the thin, old-man pajamas. He wanted to shout out after him that Sarah was gone and, who knows, maybe dead, and please, please, please, don't talk about her like that. Don't talk about her at all. Not about kids or anything we might have done together.

Bill slapped at the light switch and went into the dark living room and lay down on the couch without bothering to fold it out. He pushed at his eyes with his quaking hand.

"Some, you know, we'll see," he whispered into the darkness. What else was he supposed to say? He couldn't talk about having kids. He couldn't talk about anything now that he was alone.

As he had since the fight, Bill lay in the darkness, eyes open, watching his front door, trying to will Sarah to walk through it.

Bill was up and making breakfast when his mother came into the kitchen. She tried to take over but he gave her a cup of juice and sat her down. She sniffed audibly and said, "Are you drinking coffee now?"

"Sarah got me into it."

"I'd have hoped you'd at least try to stick with it a little while."

Bill looked to his mother sipping her apple juice. Mormons weren't supposed to drink caffeine or alcohol. "It can't make that much difference, Mom."

"That's your father talking, right through you. You might as well fix him a cup. He'll be along any minute."

They smiled at each other and he asked if they slept all right. She said they had and she asked if Sarah could join them for breakfast.

"I'll let you know when Sarah can join us," Bill said, too quickly and too loudly, and he turned away and poured the second cup of coffee. Sometimes he would tremble all over, as if with some disease normally reserved for the elderly. He could feel his mother watch him.

After breakfast Bill gave in and said he would call Sarah, to ask if she could come to lunch. He dialed his own number and pressed the phone tightly against his ear to hide the busy signal as he talked. "Can't you break away for just a little?" he asked, and waited an appropriate length of time.

"Well, all right. We'd really like to see you. But a promise is a promise, I suppose."

He waited another moment, able to hear every word she'd say, then answered, "No, no. They don't think you're trying to avoid them. They understand. It's just like a job. You can't quit just because they come for a visit."

Finally he said, "All right, honey. We'll see you later. 'Bye."

Bill took two slow breaths before saying, "She's taking the kids up to the mountains today. The doctor has a cabin up there and they're spending the weekend."

"We can stop in and see her on our way up," his mother said. "You can go up with us and then come back with her."

"I don't even know where the cabin is, Mom."

"Call her up and find out."

Bill was reaching for the phone to repeat the charade when it began to ring. His heart gave a lurching beat and he froze for an instant, feeling his parents' eyes on him. He picked up the phone and whispered hello.

As the information was given over the phone Bill's legs began to fail him. He dropped heavily into a chair at the kitchen table and finally said, "Thank you, I'll wait," and hung up the phone.

"Good Lord, Bill," his mother said, sitting next to him and touching his arm. "What was that?"

"Sarah's not baby-sitting," he said, letting out a rush of air that did nothing to fill the emptiness in his house.

His father sat down across the table. They both looked at him and waited.

Bill didn't say anything because he didn't think he could. He tried, he even lifted his head to look at his parents. They had grown old and so used to each other that his father would rather work than travel. He had married a Mormon girl forty years ago and left the East to live with her in Utah. And now he thought it would be odd to be a foreigner.

His mother had stayed home her entire life trying to have children but he had been the only one and he had moved to a foreign country with a foreign wife. Her husband and her son both drank and she knew her husband went to church just to please her and she knew her son did not even do that.

Bill felt the tears burning through his eyes and he stood quickly, his chair tipping over backward, clattering against the floor.

He'd meant to run from the room and everything else but he could barely walk to the doorway. He did not turn to face them though, until his mother whispered a question.

"Did you two have a fight, Bill?"

Bill didn't answer immediately and his mother said, "Good Lord, Bill. Everyone fights. You can't live together and not have disagreements. You—"

"We didn't have a fight," Bill said, nearly choking. It was so close to being true. "We lived together without disagreements."

"What's happened?" his father asked.

Bill gave an odd little chuckle. "She went jogging." When his parents just stared at him Bill added, "You know how she was always running. Every morning. Even when you were here for the wedding."

"Did she leave you, Bill?"

"Yes," Bill said, "she's gone." He turned back to the living room, and looked at the couch. One fight, the night before she left. Bill had slept on that couch, not because she had demanded it, but because they had always slept so closely, always touching, and neither of them had wanted to do that angrily. Bill had not slept, and when she walked out in the morning, in her jogging sweats, he thought he saw her turn in the murky light and smile at him. The smile had been like a life ring and Bill had leapt for it but she was already gone. It wasn't until that evening that he had been frightened enough to call the police, who acted as if they'd seen the same thing a hundred times before. A tiff, one of them called it.

"It'll work out, Bill. You two are so young."

"The police think they've found her," he said, the words leaking out, withering him. "They're sending someone to pick me up. I have to make a positive identification."

He saw his parents move closer together at the table, probably without realizing they had done so. He walked away from them. He stood in front of the couch but instead of sitting down he walked outside, beyond the porch, where the drizzle pattered onto his uncovered head.

If it was not raining he could see the mountains from here, blue and shimmery, like something he knew would happen, but could not yet quite see in detail. He had once pictured the future that way. If he did one thing it would lead to another, and then to another, until the entire future was laid out, blue and shimmery, just waiting for him to reach it.

The mountains would be covered with snow now though. They would still be blue, not the purple-blue of summer, but a white-blue that made them almost invisible unless the sun glinted from them. That was the way the future really was—invisible until something struck and glinted back, making everything flash so painfully clear.

Bill lifted his face to the rain. It was more a solid fog than individual striking drops. It was colder than he expected and it ran down his collar onto the warm skin of his back.

Bill looked down to the sidewalk when he heard his front door open and shut. He listened to his parents' footsteps down the walk. The steps were in unison and his mother and father circled their arms around him at the same time, three of them standing in the cold drizzle, although Bill felt it was closer to two—him alone, and his parents alone.

None of them spoke until the squad car drove into view, looking the same as it would have in the States. "Why didn't you tell us?" his mother asked then. Bill felt his father hug her. A silencing hug.

"I was hoping," Bill said.

They watched the squad car pull up before them. "I've got to go with them," Bill said. He stepped out of their reach and walked to the car. The officer leaned across the front seat and opened the door for him. Bill turned as he sat down and glimpsed his mother and father standing together in front of his house. They would be back inside by the time he returned, but they would still be together and they would still be afraid.

The fear was gone from him now. Like everyone had said, it was easier to know, even if it stole the hope. He thought of his parents sitting on the couch, looking around his empty house, too afraid to even speak. He remembered Sarah's shoes still under the couch.

The policeman spoke some kind words that Bill did not understand. He looked through the windshield, cleaned by the rain and the wipers, to where the mountains were. Up there the snow was burying things, and if the wind was still, the silence would be unlike any in the world. Maybe that was the way the future was, he thought, with the silence only broken by times he'd never even thought to hope for.

snaker

es lifted his gun and the snake leapt into the air, twisting a way snakes never do, as if trying to jump and click its heels for joy. After the snake was already dancing that way the sound of the gun slapped at me, making my eyes water. Wes surprised me like that every time he fired, moving far too quickly for a heavy old man.

When the snake was back on the ground and still, Wes walked up to it, again moving much too urgently. He toed the snake with his high boots, then bent down and snipped off the rattle. He put it in his pocket where it clicked against the pair from the other snakes.

I'd known Wes for about an hour now, and I wasn't used to this. Thinking of the gleeful, leaping dance of the snakes, I hoped we wouldn't see any more. I wondered if a snake's lot was really so awful that meeting all that hot, rushing shot could be some kind of pleasant surprise, something to click heels about.

Wes and I hadn't talked since his first shot, when he'd been telling about his thirty years in banking and I my eighteen in temperature control. We'd seen that we were too different and we hadn't put much effort into getting to know each other. Now I had to clear my throat to speak. "It's getting late," I said.

"Yes it is," Wes answered.

I nodded in the warm, dusky, winter air, watching Wes squinting intently down the road, as if there really was some vital reason to shoot these snakes. He said, "We could get my Jeep. Spotlight them in the headlights."

I wondered why in the world he would want to do that. I said, "I should be getting home, Wes. Marla's probably holding dinner."

He said, "Me too, I guess," though I knew there wasn't anyone holding dinner for him. "Spotlighting's not as fun anyway," he added.

As we walked back I searched for something to talk about, but wound up just listening to the different way Wes's boots and my running shoes crunched over the dust and rock in the desert road. Twice on our way back toward our subdivision Wes stooped to pick dead, rattleless snakes from the road and twirl them out into the creosote. He'd smile and quote my first words to him, "At least you could clean up after yourself." Even in the dying light I could see how the snakes stretched out straight and flat, gently spinning.

I ran this road every morning and I'd been the first to find the mutilated snake bodies. I'd suspected Wes, the quiet new neighbor, the old bachelor, but I'd asked around anyway. I strolled by his house several evenings, hoping to find him out on his porch. But finally I had to ring his bell and introduce myself. I told him that at first light, when I ran, the snakes looked alive enough to scare me out of my Nikes. He'd apologized, then asked me to come out with him. I hadn't been able to think of a way to say no.

When we crested the rise and were able to see the lights of our young streets Wes unloaded his gun. Phoenix hadn't made it out this far, hadn't buoyed up our land values as promised, and we were beginning to suspect it never would. We had town meetings about it. The Realtors kept assuring us though, every time they brought people in to look at the last of our model homes. I cleared my throat again and said, "I think we've been had, Wes. We've been swindled into an isolated oasis."

Wes started down the slope toward our lights and said, "I hope the Phoenicians never make it this far."

That's what he called them, Phoenicians, like they were from a different race, or time.

When we reached the first of the houses, the Haugens' adobe place, Wes dropped his gun down along his leg. It was hard to spot that way and from any of the lighted windows it would have been impossible to see. I hadn't thought of a way to ask him why he shot snakes and now I didn't ask why he hid his gun. I watched Phyllis Haugen cross her living room on the way to her kitchen.

I was relieved to reach my cul-de-sac and I told Wes to have a good night. Without pausing to talk I started away from him. He stood where I left him and said, "Come on over anytime, Mark. I go out there most every night."

He sounded awful lonely and I called back, "Sure. I will," but I walked around the bend in the road and when I knew he couldn't see me I hurried up my walk, the night gone suddenly chilly and black.

I opened our front door and the smell of something cooked with red wine wrapped around me. About a month ago, as Marla's empty days had added up, the book club had mistakenly sent *Cooking with Wine*, and now Marla was working her way through it. She called out, "Hello," when she heard the door and she came around the corner holding a spoon. "I think we've got it this time. Taste this. It's actually good."

I smiled back and sipped from her spoon. It was good, the wine not swallowed by onion or garlic or whatever had taken over the other recipes. She gave me a kiss when she drew away the spoon and I noticed her frilly apron. I shook my head and said, "Who's taken over? Harriet Nelson? The Stepford wives?"

"If you can play Daniel Boone, I can play June Cleaver," she said, twirling from my embrace, her apron spinning free. She cried, "Heavens! The dumplings!" and raced off to the kitchen.

We'd been married sixteen years and I'd never seen Marla in an apron. Until six months ago she'd been an advertising executive. I'd rarely seen her in the kitchen. "I don't think I've ever seen a dumpling," I said, trying to play along, but I didn't have any desire to see a dumpling, or an apron.

I could hear her laughing in the kitchen but before I followed her I glanced toward the picture window. Our home, so brightly lit there were no shadows, turned the window into a black mirror reflecting every detail we'd built inside—hiding everything that might be out.

Marla yelled, "So tell me about it. How did the great white hunters fare?"

I looked at myself in the window and thought of Wes out there, his gun held invisibly along his leg, and I drew the curtains, something we very rarely did. I stepped back and studied my work. The room seemed closer—cozier and safer. I walked into the kitchen and Marla said, "So? What was he like?"

I shrugged. "He kills snakes," I said. "I didn't like it."

Marla leaned back against the stove. When I didn't say anything else, she wagged her spoon impatiently. "What did he talk about? Come on, Mark. Give me the scoop."

"He didn't talk about anything." I looked up at her and laughed suddenly. "Take off that apron, for God's sake. You make me feel like I should be smoking a pipe."

"If you had slippers I'd fetch them for you."

I wanted to ask her to please stop, but I said, "Well, you should." This suburban joke of hers had run its course a long time ago.

She served up two plates and the goulash or whatever it was really was delicious. I was happy she'd pulled off a success and I told her so.

"It's eggplant." She peeked at me, waiting for a reaction.

I paused. "Eggplant?" I pushed the small chunks around my plate. "What does an eggplant even look like? A giant egg?"

She shook her head. "Nothing like an egg. It's purple. Deep, dark purple, like shiny dried blood."

"Lovely," I said, stabbing one of the pieces.

"I checked that book from front to back," she said. "Not a snake recipe in it." She looked up from her plate, smiling. "Maybe they just don't go with any local Bordeaux."

Her rhyme game. I took a deep breath, wanting to say something real, but couldn't remember how we used to talk. I said, "You'd have to cook them too slow."

"Oh, I don't know."

"Probably couldn't cut them with a hoe."

"I could try curried snake's toe."

I couldn't keep it up. I said, "You win."

"I win? Come on. Snow, blow, Merlot, *Turandot*." She threw her hands into the air and said, "I could go, and put on a show, with an absolute flow, of curried snake toe, and still not shadow, this meal's crescendo."

I whispered, "Oh, no," then threw my hands up too, in defeat, to stop the game.

Marla looked over at me. "What happened out there?" she asked. "Did he really just kill snakes?"

I nodded. "He talked a little at first. He's got a son at Stanford, general studies I think he said. And an ex somewhere. I got the impression it was recent. Probably what brought him here alone. More than anything that's what he seemed. Alone. After he shot the first snake he didn't say another word."

"Why does he shoot them?"

"I don't know. You should see him, though. It's as if his life depends on it."

"Didn't you even ask?"

I was embarrassed that I hadn't thought of a way to ask why he shot them. I said, "He's not much of a talker."

"I thought you only went to be neighborly."

"I did."

"Neighbors are supposed to talk."

"He's quiet. But he asked me to come with him again. As if he thought we'd had fun."

"Did you?"

"I didn't like the way they looked when he shot them. They danced."

Marla looked at me for an explanation but I said, "You know what he calls the people from the city? Phoenicians. Weren't they from the Bible? Wasn't Goliath a Phoenician?"

"Those were Philistines."

"I thought Philistines were art haters."

"Maybe David was a disillusioned artist."

I smiled. "He says he hopes the Phoenicians never make it down here."

"He must be made out of money then. I bet his house has devalued even since he's been here. What does he do?"

"Retired. He was into banking."

"I bet he's got a million stashed away somewhere."

"Undoubtedly," I said. I began clearing the dishes as Marla made up more details of Wes's life. She called him the Snake-Man. Snaker for short.

That was something she'd always done, glance at someone, a total stranger, and begin whispering their life history to me. The

World According to Marla, she called it. The World as It Should Be. I used to love it.

"Take off your apron, June," I said, before she could really get going. I didn't want to hear a single detail of Snaker's empty life. "I'll do the dishes."

In bed that night I picked up my magazine, but Marla held her book flat against her chest and stared into space. I waited, but when she didn't lift her book I said, "Yes?"

Marla smiled, always happy when our signals worked. For a moment she didn't answer. Then she said, "I've decided we're going to have a baby," giving a short, quick nod; the matter settled—wrapped already, a present she was giving me. Then her smile grew even wider and she turned to look at me.

"A baby?" was all I could think to say. This was from farther afield than she'd ever ventured.

"Yes. Eggplant. Get it?" She kept smiling, and when I didn't answer she went on. "We'll call her Madeline. She'll be a dazzling child, of course. She'll grow to a willowy height, possessed by a stunning yet fragile beauty that will stop talk wherever she moves."

"Oh, really?" I said.

"Yes."

I smiled a little then. It was only the game. "The World According to Marla?" I asked.

She shook her head. "The World as It Should Be. The World as It Will Be."

"We're a little old for all that."

"My clock has run down, but it hasn't stopped." She reached for me under the blankets. "We can always wind up your clock."

I didn't say anything, and she said, "Let's start now."

I turned to her, unsure now if she was playing or not. "Are you serious?" I asked.

"Oh yes. We've wasted a lot of time so far. We should get Madeline started as soon as possible. I don't want to be old and gray when the cameras pick me out of the crowd during her first Oscar acceptance."

"An actress?" I said. "How nice. And how old will she be when she collects her first Oscar?"

"Nineteen. A prodigy."

"Nineteen? And you'll be, fifty-six. Well into the Grecian Formula years."

"No time to lose."

"Marla," I said, lifting her face with my finger under her chin. When she looked at me, I asked, "Really now. Is this The World According to Marla, or are you serious?"

"I think we should have a baby," she whispered, for real.

I tried not to let my breath out in a sigh. I said, "Marla, you can't be serious."

"I am."

"We made that decision so long ago."

"We never had the operation though. We must have always known we'd change our minds."

"I haven't."

"You will."

"Marla," I said, trying to think of a way to be diplomatic, but coming up with nothing. "You're bored," I said. "A child won't change that. It'll just make you tired and bored."

Her eyes tightened, as much a sign of anger as she usually gives.

"It could even be dangerous, Marla. This late. Who knows if we could even do it?"

"Plenty of people do it."

I didn't answer, couldn't even believe we were having this talk, and Marla said, "I talked to my doctor. He said there was no reason we couldn't."

My eyes widened. "When did you do that?"

"Today."

"Oh. I see you've given this a lot of thought."

Her eyes narrowed to a squint and she glared at me a moment before flipping over, turning her back to me, edging to the far side of the bed.

I set my magazine on the nightstand and looked at the ceiling. Then I switched off the light and lay on my back on my side of the bed. "Marla?" I whispered, but she didn't answer.

"Marla," I said again, "this really isn't the best timing, you know. With you out of work, this house is taking everything we have. We don't have the extra we used to." She still didn't say anything, and I said, "Unless the Phoenicians come charging over the hill . . ."

I left it there, hoping she'd start playing with the word, but what she said was, "We've wasted so much time we no longer have *time* to spend *time* worrying about *timing*."

She'd switched words on me.

I held my breath, staring toward the dark ceiling, wondering how long it would take for this to blow over, and minutes later, out of the darkness, Marla said, "Won't you have fun out hunting snakes after you retire. I bet you can hardly wait."

It was pretty chilly in our house the next week, but over the weekend Marla began to thaw and I thought that particular storm front might have passed. But Monday morning as I was stealing out of bed for my run, Marla caught me by my shoulder and said, "Ovulation has occurred," sounding robotic, like some kind of lab technician. "The timing is correct."

When I didn't answer, she changed her voice, an impatient waitress. "Madeline says it's time to get the show on the road, Buster."

I did let out a sigh then, loud in the quiet room.

"I guarantee I'll make you burn more calories than your little run," she whispered, a seductress.

"Stop it, Marla," I said, pulling on my sweats and standing away from the bed. "We're forty years old. Babies are past us. That's the way we wanted it. It's what we decided."

Her voice caught when she said, "I'm only thirty-seven," and I whispered that I was sorry and I walked out, closing the door gently behind me.

I turned on the lights in the living room and stretched quickly, wanting to be out of the house if Marla got up. Standing from a toe touch I saw myself caught in the mirror of the picture window. The house glared empty behind me, much too bright, like an operating room. I stepped forward quickly and pulled the curtains. I thought of the reflection still there beneath the curtain and I turned off the lights too. Then I left the house, before I was finished stretching, and I started off much too quickly.

In minutes I'd left the streets and houses, trying to let my head clear, but Marla wasn't as easy to leave behind as our marooned little town site.

I crested the hill and was out in the desert, breathing hard from the first push, and I settled into my pace, trying not to think. I put my head down for the last hill and when I came over the top I nearly ran over Wes. I gave a surprised yelp and jumped to the side. Wes fell into step beside me before I had a chance to stop. "Didn't mean to scare you," he said.

I was fighting just to get my breath back and all I said was, "How are you?"

He said, "Fine," and I remembered that I never had gone back to his house as I'd told him I would.

Wes was running beside me, still wearing jeans and the same high boots he'd worn the last time I saw him. His face was glistening with sweat and I said, "This is about as far as I go."

"I know. Just a little farther," he said. "There's something I want to show you."

I was surprised and I broke stride but then trotted to catch my rhythm again. "You don't usually run, do you?"

"No. I've been up all night. I waited for you."

He turned off the road onto an old trail that led to a dry water tank I'd been to once or twice before. Wes slowed and then stopped. I ran lightly in place to keep from tightening up, but Wes breathed raggedly, bent over, his hands on his knees. We'd only run a few hundred yards but I was worried about him. He looked older than he had before.

Finally he lifted his head and pointed to the tank.

I said, "Are you all right?"

Wes nodded vigorously. "Take a look," he said, pointing at the tank again.

I peeked over the dented rim of the galvanized tank and stretched out in a neat row were the bodies of snake after snake, from about a foot long to a monster that must have been over three feet. It lay doubled back on itself in the narrow trough. I shivered and turned to look at Wes.

"Spotlighted the last five," he admitted. "But I knew I was onto a record."

"A record?"

"Fifteen. My best before that was nine. We're looking at a forty percent increase."

I stepped away from the tank and glanced up at Wes, at his proud, shy smile. He touched his bulging shirt pocket and shook it lightly. I could hear the dry, gravelly rustle under the cotton.

Although I didn't want to know a thing about him and his snakes, I asked, "Why do you kill them?"

"Why?" he asked, looking suddenly deflated, old and out of breath again. "So you won't get bit," he said, keeping his hand against the pocket full of rattles.

I stopped running in place. "I never saw a snake till you moved here, Wes."

"It was only a matter of time. They're snakes, Mark."

He paused, looking strangely shy again. "I'm always out here. I watch you turn around." Wes pointed and I looked over my shoulder at the rise where I usually turned. "That's a pretty view there. The sun coming up. First time I saw you I knew why you turned there."

"You're out here before I am?"

Wes nodded. He looked into the tank, at his snakes. "Watching you stop at the high point."

I started to bounce lightly back and forth and I looked at Wes a moment more. I said, "I've got to keep going, Wes, before I knot up."

"Sure," he said. "Go ahead. I just wanted to show you this. I'll go back in a while. I like the mornings out here."

I started away and Wes waved and kept nodding, looking into the dry trough, his face old, still sweat-sheened from the run.

I stopped for a second without planning to and said, "It's good to know you're out here, Wes," as if I had to cheer him up about something. "I sure don't worry about snakes anymore."

That was a complete lie. I'd always thought I was alone out here and I didn't like the idea that he'd been watching me for months. And I was more afraid of snakes now than I'd ever been. I'd had no idea there were so many.

Wes looked up as if he knew I was lying and I said, "I'm serious, Wes. Marla's pregnant. With a baby in town we'll need you out here full-time."

Then, before he could say anything, I started away, jogging to the rise were I usually stopped to greet the sun and run back to Marla. I didn't slow down, but picked up my pace.

Finally I was back on our quiet streets in an all-out sprint, hoping Marla was still in bed, hoping I had not yet been cast from Eden. Between the hammerings of my breath I panted, "So we're going to have a baby. She'll be a real lady."

I knew that wasn't right, but I was going too fast, trying to rhyme between breaths, and the next thing I said was, "Perhaps we'll call her Sadie."

That wasn't perfect either, and as I turned up our driveway, glancing at the curtained picture window, I remembered that her name was Madeline, and that she was going to grow to a willowy height.

concentrate

I get up earlier and earlier it seems, now that Tom's doing so much out-of-town work. I make him breakfast and maybe we'll talk a little, but mostly we're just barely awake. Before I know it he's kissing me good-bye and he's out the door. The kids are still asleep and most people would probably go back to bed then themselves, but I pour myself another cup, pinch my cheeks to keep myself awake, and use that rare time to think.

The only other time I get is while the kids are down for their naps, but some days I'm so worn-down by nap time all I can do is sit and listen to the air conditioner, wheezing and grumbling before settling into the same old routine. Shakes the whole wall when it starts. No wonder the tornadoes always blow these places wide open, when the big houses aren't touched at all. Boy, but I'd like to see one of those golf-course mansions bust open. Just imagine all the wonderful things that'd get scattered around.

Days the kids've been good, or days Tom can sleep in a little before going off to work, nap time is my real thinking time. Thinking's what's going to get us out of here. I know that. I make plans for things. I once thought how if I could design a trailer house that wouldn't get gutted so easy by tornadoes we'd be sitting pretty. But after a while I saw I didn't have the training for it. People go to schools to design buildings. Even trailer houses I suppose. So I worked at scaling down my ideas.

The next thing I tried was designing an air conditioner that wouldn't shake walls, or be so loud it'd wake you up if you happened to be lucky enough to doze some at nap time. I got so far as to getting out Tom's tools and taking apart our whole air conditioner, so I could see how it worked. But the kids got up then, before they were supposed to, and they started scrambling around in all the parts I'd taken out. I shouted at them but Tommy got hold of the fan blade and tore all around the trailer with it, pretending he was a fighter plane. He kept shooting at me and for some reason I just couldn't stand his little screwed-up face or his spitting machine-gun noises. Why did he have to keep shooting at me?

I went after him until I got him cornered in the back bedroom, but he went through the door there we never use, the fire escape door, and I had to chase him down the street through the middle of the trailer court. When I finally caught him he kept screaming, "Don't shoot me down, Mommy! Don't shoot me down!"

I wanted to paddle him so bad, but I was standing in the street then and there were a lot of women watching me, women putting out laundry, women just sitting on the steps in the heat, waiting for who knows what. Not a one of them would've thought twice about calling the police. Not that they didn't whack their own, but reporting me would've made something happen, which most everybody stuck here would've been happy for, just so they could crowd around the trailer singled out by the police car.

None of them could see Tommy was holding anything more than a toy propeller. They didn't know the first thing about air-conditioning.

I dragged Tommy back to the trailer, him digging in his heels and hollering and crying the whole way. When I launched him up the steps I was ready to light into him, but there was Jenny, our baby, sitting in all the parts of the air conditioner, teething on a black fan belt she'd wound around herself. The belt painted a big black frown down from the corners of her mouth.

I stood and stared at her, holding that dusty propeller in my hand, and I just told Tommy to go to his room. I told him to take his sister there too. He knew he was getting off light and he jumped to it. I stopped Jenny long enough to pry away the control knobs she'd balled into her fists. Then I went and sat down where Jenny'd been and I tried to gather all the parts back together. But all of a sudden it seemed like more work than a person could do and I wound up just sitting there until Tom walked through the door, after another day of work.

I knew he was doing shovel work then and that he'd be tired. But he sat down next to me and asked what had happened. I couldn't tell him one thing. Though I hated to, I just sat there and cried. I hated to let him see that. It'd worry him for days. He helped me up, and though I knew he was trying to be patient, he said, "Jesus, honey, don't you ever stop to think?" He walked me back to our bed as he talked, and when I didn't answer, he said he'd take the kids to McDonald's for dinner. Didn't even slam the door. It's no wonder they say they like him more than me.

When I got up the next morning to fix him breakfast the air conditioner was back in the wall, rumbling away, shaking half my world, and Tom didn't say another word about it. I feel about him the same way the kids do.

He kissed me and asked if I'd be all right and I said of course. Then he left like usual—before the kids got up. I watched his car disappear then peeked into the kids' room, just to see them while they were still asleep and quiet. They both had their sheets pulled clear over their heads. It gave me the shivers, and I wanted to pull the sheets down, just so they'd look more alive. But I didn't want to chance waking them any earlier than I had to and I snuck away.

As I was closing the door I noticed a poster over Tommy's bed. It was a picture of Rickey Henderson, Tommy's absolute hero, diving into second base. I figured Tom must've bought it last night, after the kids had told him their version of the air conditioner.

I closed the door, but until the kids got up I kept seeing Rickey Henderson's face, so tight with concentration, like he had to reach that base or die. I wondered if my face ever looked like that, and when the kids got up and started fighting right off, I wondered what there might be that I could dive for.

Days the breeze goes out toward the Gulf and it isn't so sticky hot, I take the kids for walks, Jenny in the stroller and Tommy just barely staying in sight. We go up to the golf course mostly. It's like our park and I let Tommy tear around and do whatever he wants while I look at the houses, wondering what's inside them. I figure if I could come up with something the people in those houses would want it wouldn't be too long before we'd have one of those places ourselves.

I was thinking on that, trying to come up with a plan, and I didn't notice when the greens on that golf course got to be too much for Tommy to resist. Four of the golf people caught him pretending he was Rickey Henderson, sliding headfirst into second. He was diving for the flag stuck in the hole, like it was a base, and when those men collared him and dragged him to me they were more than upset. They said I could be fined for what Tommy'd done. They said they paid men a lot of money to make that green just so, and that Tommy had ruined it.

I looked at them in their fine, colorful clothes and their funny shoes—men who paid other men just to grow grass—and instead of cussing them out, like I should've, I wound up laughing so hard and for so long that they all got looking uneasy, finally turning Tommy over to me and telling me not to let him loose on their course anymore. All the rest of that day I'd get the giggles and if Tommy was in reach I'd rub the top of his head. I hadn't had a laugh like that in a long time and I wanted to let him know he wasn't in trouble. The idea of those men thinking I could pay them anything they didn't already have was just too much for me.

But we kept going back up there, at first just when it was rainy and the golfers were someplace else. I wondered about the houses and when no one was around I'd go ahead and let Tommy free on the course. Sometimes I'd see him edging around a green and I'd yell out, "And Henderson's off with the pitch!" At first he used to look at me to make sure it was all right, but after he got used to it he was off as soon as I said Henderson, diving headfirst, skidding across that short, wet grass like it was plastic. Those were about the only grass stains I didn't mind working out of his jeans.

Once he slid right through the little flagpole, snapping it off clean. He came running then, his face white, thinking he was in real trouble, but he saw me laughing and as we ran away, the stroller hopping like mad over the cracks in the sidewalks, he kept asking, "Did you see me, Mommy? Did you see me?"

All that day he was wound-up that we'd been partners and when his dad came home Tommy told him about it, before I could stop him. Tom looked at me then, so hurt in his face that I knew I'd have to make Tommy stop sliding on the greens. Sometimes, without Tom saying a thing, I'd suddenly see myself like he did, not the way I always saw myself—spending all day every day in a trailer house with these two kids. I'd see what I thought was fun, the way he would, and instead of being fun anymore it'd seem stupid, even scary.

Of course I couldn't explain all that to Tommy and the next day when he kept begging me to say, "And Henderson's off with the pitch!" I wound up shouting at him. I get so mad at him sometimes, always getting me into trouble I wouldn't've even thought of myself.

But Tommy wouldn't let it go and he got so whiny and mopey I finally gave him a slap. We wound up going home before I even had a chance to look at any of those big houses. When Tom came in from work he could see right off that something'd been brewing. He took one look around, and said, "How about a baseball game? I just happen to have some Astros tickets here."

Tommy went nuts, streaking straight out to the car, and Jenny toddled out after him, thinking if he thought it was so great she better not miss her turn. I sat still, looking at Tom, at the black dirt still caked onto the knees of his jeans, the thin lines of it wrinkled into the sweaty creases of his face. He didn't have any tickets, I knew that. If he did he'd be waving them around like a bouquet.

He pulled me out of my chair and gave me a hug and said we'd pick up the tickets at the Dome. He said it wasn't any good for us to be cramped inside all through a rainy day and I went out to the car too. I didn't tell him that we went to the golf course every day now, rain or shine. One by one I was going through the things that must be in those houses, knowing something was going to come to me if I just gave it a chance. And when I figured it out I was going to surprise him with it. I could already practically see his face.

Once we got in the Dome, first thing, Tommy complained about the seats, because he couldn't even see as much as he could on TV. When he found out Rickey Henderson wasn't playing I was ready to take him out to the parking lot and lock him in the car the rest of the night. Tom tried to explain that the A's were in another league, that Henderson never played the Astros, but Tommy didn't calm down until Tom promised that we'd all ride up to Dallas some time, when the A's were taking on the Rangers.

I knew there wasn't much chance of that ever happening and looking at Tommy's sulky face the rest of the night I just wanted to shake him. Couldn't he see how it ripped Tom up to have to lie about trips to Dallas that we couldn't've afforded for anything, let alone a stupid baseball game? I decided I was going to rip his poster to shreds as soon as we got home, right in front of his face, so he could see what he was doing to his dad every day.

But on the drive home Tom went through every close play, marveling how some Puerto Rican kid could handle the ball. I saw we'd gone to that game for him too, and when we got home I put the kids to bed in a hurry, then climbed in with Tom, who was still all excited about the game.

The next morning we got up early because Tom was working clear on the other side of Houston and when we finished breakfast he said again how much fun that game had been. I wanted to ask him if he hadn't noticed Tommy the whole night, but I let it go.

Then, out of the blue, Tom started talking about money, asking how we were making out on what we had, asking how our savings looked. I handled the money for us and I said our savings didn't look like anything. I laughed and said our savings were downright invisible. He had a way of even making things like that seem fun, and I wished again that he didn't have to work so hard— that he could be around more.

He kind of poked around with his feet under the table and he said it looked like he might be having some downtime coming up, just until the hoe operator picked up his next job.

I gave a quick glance around the trailer, knowing already there wasn't a thing more we could cut back on. My eye settled on the sweating pitcher of orange juice and I said that juice was high right now, that we really didn't need it.

He laughed and said that things weren't that bad. He said he'd been having a glass of orange juice every morning since he was a kid, and he figured he'd keep on doing that. "The kids like it too," he added, patting my rear and stretching, getting ready to walk out the door. He said, "Don't worry. It's not as bad as all that." Then he kissed me and asked if I was going to be all right. Somehow that'd become part of our morning routine and I said, "I'll be fine."

As Tom drove away, I slumped back into my chair at the kitchen table. I couldn't bring myself to tackle the dishes right then. I just sat there, running my finger back and forth across the pitcher, drawing lines in the beady drops of sweat. I prayed the kids would sleep late. If they started to fight this morning I didn't know what I'd do.

That's when it hit.

Orange juice.

I sat up straight. The kids didn't like orange juice as much as Tom thought they did. I made them drink it. I made them drink the whole pitcher every day. You know how juice gets if it's left around; stale somehow, never having that same bright taste as when you first mix it up. So I always made the kids finish the pitcher, so I could make it fresh in the morning, so Tom'd at least have that before going out for another day.

It all fell together so pretty I couldn't believe it. I could see those golf people. I could see how their mornings went in their big, solid houses. They weren't like us. They didn't get up at the crack and shovel in a faceful of cold cereal. I couldn't even remember ever seeing any of them with kids. I figured they'd drink one, maybe two glasses of juice a day, tops. And they'd be in those dinky little glasses you see in stores, that aren't big enough to hold anything. A pitcher of orange juice would last forever in a house like that. Staler and staler every day.

Then, for a second, I thought, hell, those people'd just throw it away if it tasted less than perfect. But I knew people like that didn't get to live in those houses by throwing out good money. No, they'd see what I had.

It was that obvious! How long's orange juice been around? Forever, right? So long that nobody thought about it anymore. Nobody but me.

I remembered the crates of oranges they had for sale at the store. Boxes and boxes, all marked down for quick sale. Dirt cheap.

What I figured, just that quick, was that I could get a whole load of those oranges. Me and the kids could spend all day smashing them up, getting out the juice. It might even be fun for them, the way they love to smash things.

Then I'd set the juice to simmering on the stove, boiling off all the water. Making concentrate myself! It was so easy I couldn't believe it.

Once I had it boiled down I'd freeze it, but not in pitcher-size cans. No. I'd freeze it in ice-cube trays. Concentrated cubes! One bright, fresh glass of juice, perfect every single time. Nothing stale, no waste. Those golf people, the ones in the big houses, would pay for it too. They were the kind of people who'd pay big if they could see that someone had really come up with something they needed. For Chrissakes, they paid people to grow grass!

Once I proved it'd work I'd get myself a patent. Then I'd sell my world-record idea—not to Shur Fine either, but to Minute Maid maybe, one of the giants, one of the companies with the big money.

I jumped up from the table and ran to the kids' room. Jenny was awake and looking at me when I came through the door. "Come on, Hon'," I said, "we got to go to the store."

Tommy woke up as I was dressing his sister and I told him to get his clothes on. Usually he's kind of cranky first thing, but he could see something was up and he moved quick. He was sitting on the edge of his bed, trying to tie his shoes, when I grabbed his hand

and yanked him after me down the little hallway. He said a couple of times that he still had to tie his shoes, and I could feel him keep trying to bend over to tie them, even as I was pulling him out the door.

He was mad by the time we got to the car and he sat down on the ground to tie his shoes. I picked him up and sat him down in the front seat and he gave me one of his looks. I said, "You sit tight, buster. Things work out, we'll get you some of those shoes you don't have to tie."

"The ones with the Velcro?" His face lit up that quick.

"You bet," I said. I could hardly get Jenny buckled into the car seat. My key doesn't work on the driver's door but when I ran around Tommy didn't even mess with me. He leaned right over and unlocked the door. When I slid in and slammed the door behind me, he asked, "Are we running away, Mommy?"

For some reason that stole my thunder. I stopped trying to ram the key into the ignition and I turned and looked at him. "You mean without Daddy?" I said.

He just shrugged and looked away from me.

"No. Of course not," I said. "We're going to the store."

"If we're running away I want to get my poster is all," he said, nearly into his morning pout, but not quite. He wasn't sure yet what was going on—if it'd be something he'd like or not like.

"Don't you worry about Rickey," I said, finding the keyhole at last. A big blue cloud of smoke wrapped around us and I backed out. "We'll be back here before you know it."

He looked straight ahead into the dash, just like he was saying, We'll see about that. The tires screeched a little after I got it in drive and Jenny hooted.

On the way to the store I stopped at the Salvation Army. Months before I'd noticed they had a mound of plastic ice-cube trays. I remembered thinking who in the world would go to the

Army looking for ice-cube trays? But now I bought all I thought would fit in my freezer. Nickel apiece. When I threw them in the backseat Jenny picked one up and started gnawing at the corner.

At the grocery I told the guy in the white apron that I wanted oranges, boxes of them. He rounded up a couple of baggers and we filled the back of my little wagon. Cheap as they were, I was still about cleaned out at the cash register.

The man in the apron wanted to know what I was planning to do with all those oranges. "You can't freeze them," he told me.

"I know," I said.

"Making marmalade?" he wanted to know.

"No," I said, "that's been done before."

"Well what are you going to do then?"

I smiled at him, sweet, and said, "None of your beeswax." Tommy giggled.

Riding home, the three of us cramped in the front seat, the whole car filled with the smell of those oranges. It smelled like a vacation, like Florida or something, and the kids were excited and laughing the whole way.

I rumpled up Tommy's hair. "Running away!" I said. "Where'd you ever get an idea like that?" But he was embarrassed about that now and wouldn't say a word. He just pretended he didn't know what I was talking about. I never once thought of running away. But now the idea was there—foreign, but bright kind of, and shiny, like the smell of all those oranges, and I knew it wouldn't go away.

When we got back to the trailer I lugged the first couple of boxes inside and when I went out for another I found Tommy'd pulled the top off a box. The boxes were too big for them, and he and Jenny were both carrying oranges into the house, three or four at a time. Right then I could've scooped both of them into my arms for great, giant hugs. What I did was said this'd be enough and that the fun was just starting.

I got them set up at the table and gave them each an orange. I told them to roll it around, mashing it up without breaking the peel. Pretty soon they were thumping them all over the place, but they were careful about breaking them. They wanted to see what I was up to.

I pulled out the big soup pot and set it in the middle of the table. I took Tommy's orange from him and it felt like a Baggie full of water. I said, "Attaboy. Just like that." Then I cut that orange in half and the first squirts of juice splashed against the clean silver bottom of the pot. Then I rolled the halves between my palms, same way they made ropes out of Play-Doh, and the real juice slurped out.

Pretty soon Tommy got the hang of the rolling part and we were elbow to elbow over the pot. Jenny couldn't do much but bang around the oranges, but that seemed to hold her all right.

By the time we got the whole pot full we'd burned up more than three boxes of oranges. I'd hoped they'd go farther than that. The way you always add three cans of water I figured I'd have to boil it down to about a quarter of a pot before I froze it. Didn't seem like a lot of return for all that work.

I put that first pot on the stove, setting it on medium-high just to get the ball rolling. I strained out the seeds and stood and watched, stirring until I saw the first bubbles. I cut it right back to simmer then, and when I saw it'd be all right, I brought the next pot to the table and sang out, "Fill her up!"

My wrists were already tired from all the squeezing and Jenny'd given up a long time ago, but Tommy grabbed another orange and started softening it up. I was surprised to see him hang on. I asked him where Jenny'd gone and he just shrugged and kept rolling that orange around on the table.

I rounded Jenny up, her sticky hands and pudgy arms all blue and hairy from the fuzz off the carpet. I sat her back down at the table, telling her she didn't have to work, but that she had to stay here. I told her I didn't have time to be tracking her all over the place. I half-expected Tommy to squall about her not having to work, but he just held out an orange for me to cut in half. Then he started rolling the halves over the new pot, just like a pro. I would've rumpled up his hair right then, but my hands were sticky, too.

By noon we were almost done with the fourth pot and my own forearms were pretty near to being on fire—something about the rolling and squeezing that they just weren't used to. And I'd always figured I could work forever if I had to.

Tommy'd gotten awful quiet but every time I looked over he was still rolling oranges. He started doing it all crippled up though, trying not to move his wrists at all. I bent my head down low, so I could see his face, and he was biting on his lip and he had tears just started in the corners of his eyes.

I pulled the orange away from his hands and said, "For heaven's sake, Tommy. Don't hurt yourself." I took his wrists in my hands and tried to massage them a little, but he flinched.

"Your hands are too sticky," he said. "They hurt."

I looked down at my fingers and saw how our skin was stuck together, his smooth skin puckering behind my rough fingers, trying to stay with them and move the same way they did. I took my hands away and I said, "I'm sorry, Hon'. That must've felt like pulling off a Band-Aid."

"It wasn't that bad," he said, trying hard to be brave.

I set the last pot on the stove then, though it wasn't quite full. I turned the burner up to medium-high, like I'd done with all the others, just to get it going. I said, "Well, we've got all the burners filled up anyway. Nothing more for us to do for a while."

Tommy just sat at the table. I said, "I'll run you a tub. We'll soak those wrists of yours. That'll make them feel better."

"I'm all right," he mumbled.

"I know," I said. I was tired too, and I picked up Jenny and headed for the bathroom. I was proud of Tommy for working as hard as he had and I didn't want to watch him go into a sulk.

Jenny likes sitting in the tub while it fills so I sat her down and turned on the water. She started splashing and giggling and I was able to yank her out and set her on the toilet as soon as she started to pee. Normally I let her go, but I thought Tommy might want this water and I didn't think that'd be too fair after all his work.

Soon as I turned the water off and began working over Jenny with the washcloth, Tommy stepped into the bathroom. He was naked already, skinny and breakable. His arms were stained brown from the juice halfway to the elbows. He climbed right into the tub, though recently he'd started saying he was too old to share with his sister anymore.

I gave Jenny a floating duck dressed like a sailor and I started going over Tommy with the cloth. Somehow I knew that's what he wanted, to be cleaned up just like a baby, to have the nice scratchiness of the cloth rubbed over his body and to have my hands on him when they wouldn't hurt.

When I started to massage his wrists this time he didn't flinch. He asked, "What are we doing, Mommy?"

"Making orange juice," I said. "We're going to sell it to your friends up at the golf course."

He looked up at me then, to see if I was making fun of him, but I smiled and he smiled back a little. "Really?"

"You bet," I told him, massaging his palm, pulling on each of his short, thin fingers. "Does that feel good?" I asked.

He hummed an answer and nodded his head.

I gave him a little hug then and stood him up. I pulled Jenny out of the tub and wrapped a towel around her. Then I pulled the other towel from the bar and started to rub Tommy dry. "I think you're both about ready for your naps," I said.

Tommy reached down and pulled the plug and I thought I heard something else. I stopped to listen. The towel was still draped over Tommy's head and his voice was muffled when he started to say he didn't want a nap, he wanted to help.

Then I heard the noise for real: splashing, hissing, burning, and I knew I hadn't turned that last burner down and even before I'd blurted, "Goddamn it!" and started running to the kitchen the trailer was filled with a sweet, black smell that stung my eyes and made me want to throw up.

I yanked the pot from the stove and shut off the burner. The sides of the pan were scorched and I knew that was going to be a scrubbing job for sure. I dumped the pot in the sink and ran cold water into it. The burnt juice poured over the side and swirled down the drain like orange smoke.

"Damn it," I swore again. "Goddamn it to hell!"

"I didn't do it," Tommy said, quietly.

He startled me and I spun around. "For Chrissakes, Tommy. Nobody said you did anything." I said that before I'd seen him—before I'd even thought. He was just standing there, at the edge of the counter, naked, with that towel still hanging half off his head. I squatted down to be at his height and I held my arms out for him. His lip trembled some and he looked me right in the eyes and then turned and walked away.

I waited a minute, just trying to catch my breath. I stood up and ran the big spoon through the other three pots, to keep them from burning. Then I went to look for Tommy.

He was in his room, already in his bed. So was Jenny. I couldn't remember the last time that had happened without a fight. Jenny looked up at me and smiled, but Tommy had his back turned to the door and even through the sheet I could see how stiff and hard he was holding his little body. I told them to have a good nap and I shut the door before going back to the kitchen.

The smell really was enough to make me sick and I opened the door and the windows and that old air conditioner started going right away, like it could cool down the whole world. I stood and stared at it until it was over the wheezing and groaning and I shivered.

I stayed over the stove all afternoon and the kids stayed down much longer than usual. I wondered if the work'd really worn them out that much, or if maybe the smell was scaring them. I wondered if I was scaring them.

I went and checked on them once and Jenny was sitting on her bed, playing with an old Barbie she'd found a while back. It was missing its arms, but she was holding it by the hair and didn't seem to mind. Tommy still had his face to the wall. I went and sat on his bed. "I'm going to freeze the first batch now, Tommy," I said. "Don't you want to see? After you did all that work?"

"I'm sick," he murmured. "I don't feel good."

"Are you going to be all right?"

"Yes."

"Okay," I said. "I'll bring you the first glass though. That'll make you feel better."

He didn't say anything to that and when I stood up I saw him scrunch back to the far side of the bed, where he'd been before my weight had dragged him down.

Back in the kitchen I pulled the big pot off the stove and set it in the sink. I ran cold water around it, on the outside, to help it cool faster. The stuff in the pan was pretty gross looking, heavy and syrupy, but when I put my nose right down into the pot it still smelled like oranges. It was a nice smell after all afternoon with that burnt stuff in my nose.

When it was cool enough I poured it into the cube trays and slid them into the freezer. I turned the freezer all the way to the coldest. I could hardly wait to try it.

As the rest of the pots simmered down to the same gooey mess I poured them into trays and stuck them into the freezer, shifting the early ones to the top, so I could try them first. Then I sat down to start squeezing the next batch but Jenny came down the hallway and wandered over and leaned up against my leg, grabbing a fistful of my jeans. The table was a mess; dust stuck all over it from when I'd opened the windows. I'd have to clean that before I did anything and I decided I'd wait until I sampled the first batch. That'd get me going again.

So instead of going back to squeezing oranges I picked Jenny up and sat down with her on the couch. She sat there, quiet as could be with her head resting back against my chest. I could just see the top of her head and her eyelashes, sticking out longer than mine ever had. Every once in a while she'd blink and I'd know she was watching something. I looked out across the trailer; at the sticky table snatching at every bit of fluff, the piles of withered orange halves overflowing the wastebasket, the stack of gluey pans next to the sink. I wondered what in the world she could be seeing.

What I started to see were the ladies who live in those big houses. I really never had seen one of them with children. I knew some of them must have kids, but I knew they didn't ever paddle them and I knew none of their kids stayed in bed all day, saying they were sick, just to make them feel awful right when they'd been so proud.

I knew most of those ladies worked downtown in Houston, in the skyscrapers, and I knew they worked because they liked to, not because they were trying to survive. They worked like a hobby, and they made more money than I could imagine, just so they could dress up so nice every day and drive their foreign cars and be seen going in and out of those buildings made of glass.

I looked around my trailer again and thought of those women getting ready to come home. I could hear their high heels snapping against cool tile floors, and smell the breaths of all their perfumes mixing in the noiseless elevators, like an everyday trip to a flower shop. What in the world had happened to me, I wondered.

I petted the thin hair on Jenny's head and closed my eyes, waiting for my juice cubes to freeze.

Jenny fell asleep there on my lap and just before I figured Tom would get home I set her down on the couch, careful not to wake her. I went to the freezer and took out the first tray. It was frozen hard and I scratched it with my nail. An orange curl came up and I sucked it into my mouth. My whole head filled with the burning smell again and I got all loose-feeling in the bottom of my insides. I figured it was maybe just from something that was on my finger. From messing with the burnt pot maybe.

I broke out some cubes and put one into a highball glass. I filled it up the rest of the way with water and stirred it around with a teaspoon. It was sort of fun, something ordinary, but so much smaller than I was used to. It seemed to mix all right, but my hands were shaking still from that first taste.

When it was all mixed up I took a sip and instead of spitting it out, like I should've, I made myself swallow it down. I took another drink. It was all burnt up, even though I'd been so careful. It tasted like orange juice from a forest fire. Drinking it down I could feel it filling me up with all the ashes of everything I'd planned.

I looked around the house, which I'd meant to get cleaned before Tom came home, when I was going to give him his single-serving glass of orange juice. I set my glass on the counter but I missed and it crashed to the floor. If it'd been real glass it would've shattered all over the place.

That woke Jenny up and she started to whimper and when I just walked away she got mad and began to cry for real. I went into the kids' room and I caught Tommy flipping over so his back was to me again. I walked over to his bed and got right in there with him, curling myself around his toasty, naked body.

Tommy didn't turn around or soften up one bit and the last thing I saw before I closed my eyes was Rickey Henderson, so close to that base and safety, but frozen in midair, his face forever twisted in concentration and effort.

I didn't cry. I was afraid of what would happen if I ever started that. I only held Tommy tighter and tighter, trying to melt him. And just before I heard Tom pull up and walk through the door, Tommy finally started to relax. I told him I was sorry about everything I'd ever done to him. He didn't say anything but he started to play with my fingers, where they were wrapped around his chest. He twisted my wedding ring back and forth, like he used to when he was such a little boy.

My mouth was right against his ear and I whispered again that I was sorry. Then I heard Tom come in and I heard his low whistle when he saw the kitchen. I could hear him pick up Jenny, who was still whimpering alone on the couch.

He said, "Where's Momma, Sugarbaby?"

I heard Jenny laugh and I knew he was tickling her, but I could hear the nervousness in his voice. You can hear everything through these walls. I heard Jenny say I was in her room, sleeping with Tommy. Tom asked if we were sick and Jenny said, "No."

When Tom said, "Well, let's go see if we can wake them up," I couldn't hold back the tears anymore and I whispered into Tommy's ear that I loved him and that he should never ever be afraid that we'd run away.

When he squeezed my arms tighter to his chest I opened my eyes and saw Rickey Henderson again, in mid-dive. But for the first time I noticed—blurred and in the background—the umpire in his black suit, legs spread wide and low, his arms already starting out to his sides, giving the safe sign.

helmets

A s our buses rushed into the desert I sat alone in my seat, nearly
lulled to sleep by the endless flitting of the sagebrush and the
mingling conversations of the other engineers. The sun had just
begun to rise at our backs when suddenly, apparently out of
nowhere, the Helmet family appeared.

I didn't sit up any straighter at first—a car, after all, while
rare this far out, is not unheard-of. But as it passed, going in the opposite direction, toward town, I caught a glimpse inside. And what
I saw was a family; father behind the wheel, mother at the other
door, son and daughter occupying the rear seat. Tediously normal
if it were not for the fact that everyone in this family wore helmets.
Not steel military issue, but flashy white things. Most likely nothing
more substantial than bicycle helmets. I did sit up straighter then,
turning to stare, though by then the car was already long gone.

For a moment I simply gazed at the empty road. Then I
glanced around the bus for someone I might tell about what I'd
seen. But, with my coworkers an entire generation younger than
myself, I rarely spoke on those long rides. So I settled back into my
seat, making a mental note to tell Nancy about this strange family
that evening during dinner. What in the world did they think they
could protect themselves from?

After arriving at the facility a small crisis in the magnetic-containment project kept our team in meetings most of the day. I sat quietly through all of them, wishing I'd been left to work alone at my computer, never being quick enough to think of much to add to these lightning brainstormings. There was a great worry over the possibility of unwanted detonations but since my earliest days with DOE we've had a nearly unblemished safety record and I wasn't able to muster the same concern as the young men around me. These things always worked out. Instead of listening, I found myself wondering about that family and their helmets, nearly smiling as I imagined how an unwanted detonation would certainly ruin their safe day.

When the meetings finally wrapped up the team broke into its usual groups, leaving me to get back to my workstation. I'd just flipped on my monitor when my supervisor, Mr. Becker, a thick-haired man half my age, blocked the exit to my cubicle. He smiled and asked if I'd had a chance over the weekend to consider our talk about early retirement.

Glancing at the monitor's cool blue I slipped my hands beneath my legs. "Nancy and I discussed it, of course," I began, but I couldn't think of another word. Picking at the sturdy weave of the upholstery beneath my fingers I started over. "Perhaps after ironing out some of this magnetic containment . . . ," but Mr. Becker interrupted, assuring me that my work had been invaluable, but adding with a small laugh that he thought they'd be able to muddle on, although, of course, I'd be sorely missed.

With a light slap on my shoulder, a habit of his I could barely stand, he asked me again to give it some serious thought. Before I knew it we were all hustling out to the buses for our sixty-mile ride back to civilization.

I picked at my dinner that night, Nancy waiting patiently to hear what was bothering me. She knows I'm not allowed to discuss my projects and at times that has been more helpful than I'd care to admit. But tonight she kept waiting and finally, setting my silverware aside, I said, "Do you remember, Nancy, how exciting everything was when I first started?" Naturally, I'd been thinking a lot about those early days, when even the hush-hush nature of the work seemed to add a flair my life had never known.

"Of course," Nancy said, smiling. "Phyllis threw us the bon voyage party. As if Idaho were in another country."

"Public Relations has replaced the boundary signs again," I said. "INEL this time. Idaho National Engineering Laboratory."

Nancy's smile began to falter but I continued. "Much less threatening than the Department of Energy Test Site, I suppose. But they've left up the military's 'No Trespassing' signs, and the 'Unexploded Ordnance Area' notices. Who do you suppose they think they're fooling?"

Nancy didn't answer and I said, "Do you remember when Congress gave us all the money we could ask for? When people still thought we were doing something essential? When it wasn't something to try to hide, to be embarrassed about?"

I realized I'd raised my voice, but Nancy's eyes met mine. "Those were the exciting years," she agreed, "when everything was so dangerous." But then, lowering her voice to a whisper, she added, "We made a world so dangerous we wouldn't even risk bringing children into it. How could I forget?"

When I didn't answer Nancy quietly raised her plate, asking for more.

"I don't know what's the matter with this country anymore," I muttered, but I forked a thin slice of ham onto Nancy's plate.

It wasn't until I saw the same family the very next day, again helmeted against the world, that I realized I'd forgotten to tell

Nancy about them. I reminded myself all day long, and that evening, as soon as we were settled in for dinner, I said to Nancy, "I've seen the oddest thing the past two mornings."

Nancy raised an eyebrow.

I filled her plate and passed it to her. "A family," I continued, "in a car. Coming to town as I go to work."

She listened quietly, a smile waiting to start at the corners of her mouth.

"Every one of them," I said, pausing, letting the suspense build as I served myself, "mother, father, son, daughter—every one—wears a helmet. Every day."

"Helmets?" Nancy asked, her smile breaking across her face, sure she was being teased.

"Helmets!"

"What in heavens for?"

I shrugged hugely. "They must believe it offers them some sort of extra protection. Something the rest of us don't have." My eyes widened in disbelief, accenting the mockery in my voice.

"You can't be serious, Wilton."

"I am though," I said, smiling myself as I picked up my fork. "Can you believe the naivete of some people? Why, with even our oldest projects we could leave nothing of them but white shadows on the road! Helmets!"

Nancy looked at me then, her fingers picking at an ironed wrinkle on the tablecloth, her mouth for a moment as tight as the line in the material. She dipped her head to her dinner and when she looked back up she said they'd started a new program at the grade school where she volunteered. "The MAN project," she said it was called. "Men Are Nice. Some of those children have never known a man who's done anything but abuse them or their mother." She looked at me, shaking her head. "We're looking for men to read stories to them after school. Men just to be kind."

I nodded, but the change of subject wasn't lost on me. Nancy has never liked me talking about my work.

The family was there again the next morning, and the next, so regularly I ceased to be surprised by their appearance. In fact, I sat in my seat in the INEL bus and waited for them, tense until their little white sedan rolled past, their helmets flashing white inside. Only then did I ease back into my seat to begin pondering the day's tasks.

This went on for an entire week before I realized the family had begun to interrupt my thoughts even while I worked. I would find myself suddenly woken as if from a trance, staring into some unfinished design on my monitor, realizing I had only been wondering about that family and their silly helmets. Often I would have no idea how much time had been lost.

While perhaps I was never the Department's most brilliant design engineer I was always steady and I was frightened to find myself so easily distracted. The collapse of the Cold War undoubtedly sapped some urgency, but even last month, though deeply shaken after first being interrogated about my interest in early retirement, an interest that is absolutely nonexistent, I was back on task within minutes.

The following morning I listened to the young engineers discuss the newest round of layoffs until I saw the car rolling carefully toward us. As it hugged the shoulder, anticipating our line of buses streaking by, my mind suddenly filled with all the things we could do to their car and their preposterous notions of safety. The stark white outlines left by a nuclear flash weren't even necessary. We had the technology now to blow them into the air first, then atomize them, leaving not a trace of their vain hopes.

As soon as the car swooshed by, however, these thoughts left me quite shaken. I rarely allow myself to dwell upon the use of our work, particularly not in any way so personal or inappropriate. I decided I would have to track down the Helmet family, as Nancy had begun to call them, to see exactly what it was that they thought they could keep so safe.

The very next morning I purposely missed my bus. Feigning annoyance for Nancy's sake, I scrambled into our car and raced out for the desert, hoping to find a spot to wait until I could follow the Helmet family to wherever it was they went. For the first time ever I fabricated an excuse to explain my absence from work.

I'd just gotten turned around when the white sedan came over the hill, right on schedule, moving completely into the other lane as they went around me, as if I might fling open my door and step blindly into their path—completely unaware of the concept of safety. I pulled out and followed them into Idaho Falls.

The trailing was more difficult in town with the stoplights and traffic. My heart was pounding from a wild acceleration through a mostly yellow light when the white sedan first pulled over. They were in front of a school and I had to stop in the bus area. I watched as the daughter, probably no more than ten or eleven years old, hopped briskly out and started for the playground, already crowding with children.

She glanced over her shoulder, a slim, pretty, breakable child, long black hair flowing from beneath her helmet. Following her glance I saw her parents' car pulling back into traffic, but I hesitated. The girl was already working on the helmet's chin strap, peeling the helmet from her head and running her fingers through her hair to remove its crushing outline. She hid the helmet in her backpack and swung through the gateway bars of the playground, where she disappeared in a group of laughing girls.

The blare of the bus horn startled me so greatly I jerked forward without checking traffic, causing another, smaller, horn blast. A mother glared, the seats of her car filled with wide-eyed children. At the first available corner I signaled and turned away, fleeing, having lost the white sedan during my study of their daughter—their daughter who didn't share their hopeless ideas of safety a second longer than necessary for appearances.

After driving pointlessly for several minutes I headed back for the school. I wanted again to see that young girl, so like all the others, so childish looking, but already able to see with a clarity greater than her parents.

But at the school the playground was empty, the children all safely inside, even the crossing guards heading for their cars, not to return until the lunchtime recess.

I didn't go to work that day, though I would have been little more than an hour late. For a long time I simply circled through town, hoping somehow that I might bump into the white sedan.

I considered going home, spending the day with Nancy, but I pictured sitting on the edge of the bed while she dressed for her afternoon at the school, clipping her earrings on, only half-listening to the excuse I'd invented to explain being home in the middle of the day. Once she was gone I'd walk through our house, my footsteps ringing off the hardwood floors, wondering for the first time how she filled all the hours.

It was nearly dark before I stopped my car in our driveway and spent the dinner hour telling Nancy what I'd accomplished at work that day.

The following morning I again walked around the corner as if going to work. After waiting an appropriate time I returned home for the car keys, grumbling about missing the bus. But this morning Nancy followed me out to the driveway. "Wilton?" she said, leaving it there for me to explain.

"What?" I asked, irritated by being forced to play simple.

"I don't remember you ever missing the bus before." She looked at me carefully, truly concerned. "Is everything all right? Everything at work?"

Ever since Mr. Becker had gone past the suggestion stage I'd tried to come up with some way to tell Nancy about what they were still calling "early retirement," though "forced" seemed considerably more accurate. But, after so long a time believing in my work, I didn't know what to say. I smiled at Nancy and shook my head. "Old-timer's disease," I said.

She smiled obediently, but it did little to dispel her worried expression. "You'd tell me, wouldn't you, Wilton? If there was something?"

I said, "Of course I would, Nancy."

She watched me back down the drive and even after I turned the corner I could feel her watching.

Worrying that people as careful as the Helmet family would surely recognize the same car following them in from the desert, I decided to wait for them at the daughter's school. My timing was off, perhaps due to my excitement, or my rush to get away from Nancy's questions, and I spent nearly half an hour parked in front of the school before the white sedan appeared.

I watched the girl repeat her movements of yesterday, as far as the unstrapping of the helmet, before I had to leave to follow the rest of her family. As I chased them across town I wondered if the parents were at all aware of their daughter's duplicity. Or perhaps she was allowed to remove her helmet in school. Perhaps her parents were so adept at self-deception that they could imagine school as a safe haven, despite the contents of the nightly newscasts.

The car stopped at another school and even as I pulled in, several slots behind them, I wondered why the children attended different schools, schools so far apart. I had not yet had time to take in my surroundings.

Rather than the son simply leaping from the car as their daughter had, both front doors swung open. I nearly smiled at the recklessness of the move, the helmeted father actually stepping into the traffic lane. They met at the son's door and opened it for him. Then together they helped him toward the school door, his steps herky-jerky, decisionless, his head rolling this way and that, sometimes lolling as if its weight was simply too much for the thin neck.

Realizing what I was seeing, I averted my gaze, wiping at my forehead's sudden sheen of sweat, feeling little more than a Peeping Tom. Instead, I looked into the playground, awash with adults, more of them, it seemed, than children. Nearly all the children wore helmets, some much more severe than the son's white model, some heavy and leatherish, some even with face guards, though the children never seemed out of catching range of an attendant, should their labored steps disintegrate into complete collapse.

At the door, as the parents stooped to kiss and pet him, I saw the unmistakable cast of the son's face, the mongoloid features of whatever it is that causes all that.

The family disappeared inside for just a moment, then the parents reappeared alone, trotting to their car, hands fiddling with their chin straps. At the car they flipped their helmets into the still-open door of the backseat. The father grazed a finger along his wife's shoulders as he moved around her on his way to the driver's seat and, though I'd planned to follow them, to see where they went next, I knew it was no longer necessary. I stayed where I was for quite some time, trying not to look into that awful playground, the white flash of the son's helmet unmistakable in the mass of globed heads.

I sat with my head down and my eyes closed until I'd re-
gained some composure—an old trick of Nancy's—and then I eased
into the street, wondering where to go. The quick tire screech was
all the warning I had before the jolt and the sound of the metal.

The woman was kind—flustered, but kind, more concerned
with her helmeted daughter than any minor damage to her station
wagon. I tried to give cash, but she laughed, saying a swap of in-
surance papers would be plenty. She seemed surprised not to know
me, and was immediately standoffish when I said I wasn't here with
a child. I followed her glance to the playground, where the atten-
dants were trying to keep their flock from stumbling toward the excitement of our accident. I wondered for a horrified moment if
there were people who actually came to gawk at these children and,
without planning to, I said, "I'm new here. I'm still just checking
into schools for our child."

I accompanied her all the way up the steps with her girl as
she assured me that I could do no better than this school. The parents too were wonderful. And the support groups, if we were inter-
ested in that sort of thing. I said that indeed we were, my wife and
I, and we formally introduced ourselves before returning to our
cars, where I apologized once more.

I made it several blocks before pulling over and again lowering my head and closing my eyes.

I don't know how she managed it, if she was waiting by the
window since I left or not, but Nancy was on the front step before
I'd finished pulling into the driveway. Coming home in the middle
of the morning, with the fender buckled, I knew there would have
to be some explanation, but I'd been unable to collect my thoughts
even toward a starting point.

Nancy met me at the car door, nearly blocking me in.
"Good morning," I said, sliding out and stepping around her to-

ward the house. She was already dressed for her volunteer work with those children who'd never met a nice man.

"Wilton?" she said, following. "What is it, Wilton?"

I was sweating and my hand trembled as I reached for the doorknob.

"What happened to the car, Wilton? Have you been hurt?"

At the edge of the dining room table I glanced around our modest house and then turned and looked at Nancy, my wife of thirty-seven years. "They're forcing me to retire," I said, out with it all at once.

Nancy stared. "But the car? Are you all right?"

I waved that away. "Retired," I repeated. "I'm going to lose my work."

"I know how much your work means to you, Wilton," she said quietly. "But that doesn't explain this. What's happened?"

"I've been following the Helmet family," I said, surprising myself. "The helmets. They're not for what we thought. That family knows more about safety than we ever will." Suddenly I needed to sit down. "My work, Nancy. It's all I've ever had."

"What about the Helmet family?" she asked, pulling up one of the dining room chairs and sitting beside me.

Briefly I told her what I'd seen, how they wore the helmets only so their boy wouldn't be alone. I even told about the woman who'd hit our car. "I had to lie to her," I said. "She thought I was just there to stare at those pitiful children."

"What did you tell her?" she whispered.

"I told her we had our own child. That I was simply looking for a place where he'd be welcome."

As I spoke Nancy broke down and I held her and rocked her in those hard dining room chairs, my head down over hers, my eyes closed tight.

headwaters

'm not as sure about anything as I am that I love my wife. This is Rock-of-Gibraltar stuff. Gene, at work, if I ever told him that, which I never would, would say the only things you can be sure of are death and taxes. I know he'd say that. It's the way he talks. But he'd be wrong. I understand that death will come, but it's pretty easy not to think about it. And taxes. You can always just stop paying them, run the risk. But it's not possible for me to stop thinking about Kim. That wouldn't be a risk. It'd be suicide. I think about her all the time.

So, I can barely stand it when she has to travel for work. It's only once or at the most twice a year, usually not for more than a week or two. Even so, I get nervous just thinking about it, because, behind everything, there's this feeling that creeps into me as the day of her departure grows closer. A feeling I can't stop. A feeling of anticipation. It gets so I can't wait to be alone.

Last year it was only to Billings, a three-and-a-half-hour drive from our home in Great Falls. She got a motel room right on the Yellowstone and I drove down for the weekend. We spent a day on the river and she was back home before I knew it.

But this time the bank's sending her to the main office in Minneapolis. For a month. Training on the new system. We've talked about my flying out for a weekend but know we can't really afford that kind of trip.

A month alone. I barely know what to do with myself, even what to think. I hold Kim at night and tell her I'm going to miss her, which is the absolute truth. She hugs back and says she'll miss me too, but that it's only a month and that we'll call. We say it'll be like before we were married, the year she was still in school in Colorado. I know all that. I can hardly wait.

At the airport I check to make sure she'll have a rent-a-car waiting. The bank would pick her up, of course, but she likes to have that mobility, and I like the idea that she'll be able to see some things, that she won't be trapped in a motel room alone the whole month. The last few nights we've looked through the road atlas together, and though it's a long drive, she's decided she's going to drive over to Lake Itasca. She says she's always wanted to see the headwaters of the Mississippi. Hearing her say that I wish I could see it too—the very beginning of something so huge.

She hugs me hard at the entrance to security and we kiss. "I'll call when I get to my room," she says. I nod and give her shoulder one more squeeze and she passes through the gate without a beep. She picks her bag up from the conveyor belt and waves once more. She's pulling out her book when I turn and start for the escalator.

The airport is already different, now that I'm leaving alone. Above the escalators is a huge mural of Lewis and Clark, the great explorers, portaging their heavy wooden boats around the great falls of the Missouri. It took weeks.

When I get in my car I drive carefully, wondering which turns to take. I can do anything now and each intersection offers a choice. I drive past the turn to our house, though in the late evening like this the light streaming in the bay window would be golden, the kind Kim likes to sit in and read.

I reach the north edge of town and turn toward the old road to Canada, still called the Bootlegger Trail. But, at last, I drive past the trail, staying on the highway. I roll down the window and step on the accelerator. Just out of town I'm driving eighty-five, laughing. We never drive crazy.

I turn at the little road to the dam and take it easy. The road's so bad here I couldn't speed if I wanted to.

The sun's sinking fast as I drop down the bluffs to the river, past the power-company houses. I walk over the suspension bridge to the island and look upriver to the immense concrete wall looming over the terraced drops of rock that used to be the great falls. There's still a little water making the drops, but though the sun is already down behind the dam, it's still bright, making it hard to see. I turn to the island and think of Kim up in the sky now. Six miles high with the sun still on her, while I'm grounded here with the dark closing in.

We were married here, on this island, with our backs turned to the turbines and generators while the preacher read the words. When Lewis and Clark came through here they'd heard of the falls from the Indians who knew the land ahead. They knew what to expect, what lay before them. Then they'd seen the falls, from miles away, just by the plumes of mist rising out of the dry plains. Lewis had gone on ahead, to make sure, maybe pretending there could possibly be some other explanation, some way they could keep using the river without having to carry everything around this overwhelming obstacle.

It's still one of our favorite places, but as I walk back to the car I glance once more at the wall of concrete and think of the plume that had guided the explorers. It's hard for me to believe that anything could hold all that back, even men and concrete.

As I climb back up the banks onto the flatland of wheat and head home, I wonder if I would have raced out here for no reason if Kim had been home. I wouldn't have, not without picking her up first.

I park in our garage and walk through the back door. "Honey, I'm home!" I yell, smiling, knowing there'll be no answer. I think about dinner but decide to skip it. Instead I walk around our empty house, finally sitting down in my favorite chair, a wing chair that'd belonged to Kim's grandmother. I pick up a book Kim left out. Opening it to the first page, I begin to pretend I'm not waiting for her call.

I've dozed before the phone rings and I wake up startled. It's later than it should be and I answer the phone saying, "What took you so long? I've been worried sick." It's a joke.

I recognize Gene's voice immediately. Gene from work. He says, "Thanks for caring."

"Hi, Gene," I say. "I thought it was Kim." I hear a lot of noise in the background.

"Kim's long gone, Ted. I'm down here at Thirsty's. Thought I'd drag your single butt down with me."

"I'm beat, Gene. Already in bed. But thanks."

"Maybe tomorrow," Gene says. "After work. I'll see you then. Try not to worry yourself sick about me."

The phone goes dead, but I know Gene will keep asking, all month, thinking he's being a friend, helping me over this separation. Tomorrow at work I'll have to come up with another excuse. Since his divorce Gene hasn't been somebody to go out with, not unless you can cut it short. Once out he acts as if he has no home to go to.

While I sit thinking about Gene the phone begins to wail its off-the-hook warning and I hang up quickly. I walk through the house again and decide I might as well get into bed. I slip under the covers and sit up, making sure I can reach the phone easily, then I lay back down, fluffing the pillow for my head. It's unusual to have all that bed and I lie diagonally, filling all the space I can.

Kim doesn't call until the next morning. I'm out of the shower, shaving, and I answer wearing just my towel. They'd met her at the airport and insisted on taking her out. She'll rent the car later, she tells me, on the weekend. After looking at the schedule she saw she wouldn't have a chance to use it before then anyway.

I tell her I didn't sleep all night, I was so worried about her.

"I bet," she says. "I can practically feel the sheet wrinkles on your cheek from here."

"Worry lines," I call them.

She says she's got to run to some kind of breakfast meeting, and she says, "Love."

I say the whole thing, "I love you," and she says, "Thanks," like she always does, though I've told her time and time again that she doesn't need to thank me, that it's not something I can even control.

At work, as the day grows shorter, I spend most of my time dodging Gene. I don't like the idea of having to make something up to avoid going out with him and I wind up leaving fifteen minutes early, when I see him head down to mailing.

It's not that I dislike Gene. Fixing myself dinner, cutting tomatoes from Kim's garden, I understand for the first time that he makes me uncomfortable simply because he is so terminally alone. His solitude floats around him like a fog.

I go heavy on the curry, a spice Kim can't tolerate. I've got one of my old Springsteen tapes on too, and I'm singing along. It's up so loud I can't hear myself. He sets Kim's teeth on edge.

I turn the stove to simmer and walk into the living room to get the full effect of the speakers, but the tape is over and I walk into silence. I'm playing at solitude, I realize, so safe in the knowledge that the game will end that it isn't even fun. I walk around the house and wonder what I'll do next, now that I can do anything I want.

I give Kim a call but she isn't in. After dinner I read a while. Kim still isn't in when I call again, and I feel sorry for her, knowing how they stack on the dinners and the social stuff at the beginning of these conferences. She's always hated those kinds of things. Finally I call Gene but he isn't home either.

Over the next few weeks I talk to Kim several times; all the usual stuff and she does most of the talking, because things have been going on with her. I'm just holding down the fort. I tell her I'm sick of curry and Springsteen both and she laughs.

Toward the end of the month she calls early one morning and tells me that she's finally managed to free herself for the last weekend and she's leaving right after work on Friday. She's going to see the Mississippi's headwaters.

I think of all our drives together and how I almost always do the driving. I ask, "Did you find anyone to go with you? To share the driving?"

"And waste this time by myself?"

I say, "Be careful then."

"It's hardly more than a trip to Billings. You should listen to the people here though, Ted. They act as if I'm driving to the moon."

"There are a lot more people on the roads there. If you get tired, find yourself a motel. Just be careful."

"I will be, Ted. We always are. I'll give you a call. Maybe write you a postcard."

She's winding up and when she says, "Love," I say, "Love," back and she says, "Thanks," then, "Bye."

I hang up and smile. "You don't have to say thanks," I say out loud to myself. But I'm thinking about her driving now, cars moving fast, and the smile won't keep those away.

Our accident was years ago and I haven't thought of it in a long time. But suddenly, holding the receiver down on its cradle, I can hear the instantaneous rushing pop of inflating air bags. We'd paid extra for the double bags, knowing even then how fragile some things are.

I leave the phone and sit down in Kim's grandmother's chair. We were driving home, only blocks from our house, joking about something—I can no longer remember what—but I took my hands off the wheel for an instant, like anybody's done one time or another, shaking them wide for emphasis. And that's when the car crossed the line and struck us head-on. We were laughing and looking at each other and neither one of us saw it happen.

We weren't going very fast, twenty, maybe even fifteen, but so was the other car, and the speeds combined and as soon as I heard the metal buckling and the glass breaking I knew exactly what was happening. But, in the middle of all that, I caught the whop of air into the bags and I remember thinking, "What's that?"

We bounced back away from the bags and then we weren't moving anymore. We were still looking at each other and we asked, "Are you all right?" at the same time, and we both answered, "I think so," at the same time and that let us laugh.

I hadn't even turned away from Kim before there was a man at my window, nearly sobbing, saying it was his fault, asking if we were okay.

It wasn't until we started trying to get out of the car, when I went to undo my seat belt, that I realized my fingers were broken. Spread wide they'd missed the air bag and the force of the crash had thrown them into the dashboard. They stuck out at funny angles, all four on each hand. I said, "Kim. My hands are broken," and she did my belt for me and we sat down on the curb and waited for an ambulance. She held her arm around me the whole time, though my hands hadn't quite started to hurt yet. We didn't really need an ambulance. If the car had worked Kim could have driven me to the hospital herself.

The other driver paced frantically, apologizing, saying it was his fault, like that would do something for him. Every once in a while he would stop in front of me and say, "Oh man, look at your hands."

I didn't want to look at them and I'd say, "They're okay. They don't even hurt."

While I sat comforting the driver, Kim kept hugging me, feeling so bad about my hands she couldn't talk, and I gazed out into the street, at our crushed cars only feet away. They were both in my lane and I knew the driver was right, that it had been his fault, but I began to shake. I thought of how I'd been driving with Kim next to me, how I hadn't even been holding on to the wheel, hadn't even been looking at the road.

I look down at my fingers now, where they grip the arms of the wing chair. Only one required surgery and you have to know where the scars are to see them right off. When we got home from the hospital, my fingers splinted and wrapped until my hands were giant, gauzy clubs, each with its own heartbeat, Kim started to wait on me. Once the pain was gone she joked about my leaving the bandages on far longer than was necessary. "I think you're getting awfully used to this hand-and-foot service," she'd say.

I really wasn't though. I played the jokes, but I didn't like the helplessness, which is easy enough to believe. What I really hated was her waiting on me. I didn't like seeing her like that and I only wanted things to get back to the way they'd been before.

Finally I lied to her, making her unwrap my hands before their time and I started using them too soon. The doctor lectured me and there were complications in the one finger, the one they finally operated on. I still can't feel things with the tip of that finger, though I've never told Kim that. Sitting in the chair, I tremble, still not quite believing I'd let go of the wheel that way.

I go to work but I keep thinking of Kim driving that far without me and I don't get much done. In the afternoon Gene asks me to go out with him again. I've gone a few times since Kim's been gone, when I haven't been able to avoid it, and I've really kind of enjoyed it. Gene's not a bad guy.

But I've enjoyed it because I've been eavesdropping, or peeping maybe, on a life I don't have. I've enjoyed myself because I've gone to my empty house afterward knowing it wasn't really empty—because I've known all along that that's where I'd be going. I tell Gene I can't go with him tonight.

"What's up?" he asks.

"Nothing really, I just won't be able to make it."

Gene grins, a grin I don't like, and says, "Becky asked about you last night."

I wonder which one of the women who'd sat at our tables was Becky. "No can-do," I say. It's the way Gene talks. Death and taxes.

"Brick shithouse," he says, leaving it open, and I remember who Becky is.

I shake my head, thinking of Kim driving with all her concentration, hands tight on the wheel. And suddenly I realize that even though I'm only playing at this aloneness game, it's a game that it really is possible to lose. Before I know what I'm saying I tell Gene, "I've got to pack tonight."

"Pack? For what?"

"I'm going to Minneapolis for the weekend." I think of how we'd already decided we couldn't afford this. I make up my plan out loud to Gene, practicing for when I'll tell Kim. "We're trading in Kim's return fare and driving back. We're going to the headwaters of the Mississippi."

"You're driving a thousand miles for fun?"

"Both of us. One long Sunday drive."

Gene shakes his head, then says, "Crazy as a coot," and I tell him to say hello to Becky. It's time to go and on the grease-board calendar I draw an *X* through the next five days of my row. I write "Family Emergency."

I fill the car at the station near the office, check the oil and all the rest. At home I throw some things together, things for both of us, things she wouldn't have packed for a business trip. Then I stop at the phone and give her a call. She's not in and I ask for her to be paged. I identify myself as her husband, liking the sound of it. I'm told she's in a meeting and I wind up saying there's an emergency. They agree to bring her to the phone and I ask them to let her know it's nothing desperate, nothing to be afraid of yet.

I have nearly five minutes to come up with an explanation, but I don't get it fit into words before I hear the quick jostle of the phone. She asks, "Are you all right?" and I try to say the same thing at the same time, picturing her in the car seconds after the crash, her eyes wide, her hair thrown forward over her face, waiting to laugh as soon as we say together that we are, indeed, all right.

She says, "What?" and I say, "We need to go to the headwaters together," and she says, "What?" again.

I begin to explain and when I'm done she asks if that's what I took her out of a meeting for, if that's what I scared her half to death for. I say, "Yes," and she says, "I love you." Not even the shortened version.

I say, "Thanks."

"You don't have to tell me that," she says, and I practice the circle of my fingers around the ring of the steering wheel, where I swear they will always stay. The scarred finger is stiff and won't quite make the proper curl.

"I've got to go," she says, and I say, "It's fifteen hours. I'll see you tomorrow night."

She says, "Be careful," and I say, "You know it."

Then we're hanging up the phones and I'm walking. Walking quickly out of our empty house. In seconds I'm driving east out of Great Falls, where the plume once rose out of the calm, flat plains, warning travelers of what lay ahead.

s a g e
a n d
S A L T

'd walked out of my folks' trailer court in Chugwater, Wyoming, a million times. Only this time I'd decided to keep going. I walked fast, through the empty streets and past the most popular building in Chugwater, a windowless cinder-block bar called the Tahiti Lounge. Ten o'clock in the morning and a friend of my dad's was going in. When he opened the door to the darkness inside I started to run, my tiny pack slapping against my back, full of everything I thought I might need.

At the highway there was nothing but bare pavement stretching flat and empty in both directions. Nothing around me but air, and I still felt that close to smothering. I stopped running and tried to catch my breath.

The sky was full of the usual summer clouds—dry, white, billowy things, like old-time pirate ships with all their sails out and going. I walked along the shoulder, careful of my footing, watching the scuffed toes of my cowboy boots. "Walk the plank, matey," I said out loud to nobody.

The first car to come along startled me but it pulled over, and looking at its brake lights I finally took a real taste of the sweet, flat basin air that had surrounded me my whole life. I froze, glancing back at the little cluster of buildings I was leaving.

Chugwater was nothing but a pinprick, a thing I wouldn't've even noticed if it hadn't drawn blood, but I stood there looking at its empty, wind-blasted streets, its fences full of tumbleweeds stopped in their tracks, and I didn't move. I looked back at the car idling on the shoulder a hundred feet away.

Its brake lights winked out and I thought of those clouds racing away, looking so proud and clean, and I ran for the car. The lights came back on and the side door swung open. I slammed it behind me and as we built up speed the driver asked where I was headed. It took me a second to come up with an answer. "West," I said.

The sun came hot through the windshield and as we drove I stared out, watching the Medicine Bows get bigger, then slide back behind me and disappear. I'd spent my whole life thinking those mountains were the edge of the world. I sank deeper into the car seat and practiced breathing without gasping.

The only thing I felt funny about leaving was my folks. They weren't monsters or anything. I just couldn't bear to see them anymore. I couldn't take the chance of looking like that someday myself—zombyized, going back and forth to the oil fields, like they could give life or air or something.

It took a while, but I wound up going clean out to the coast, to Seattle. On the road everybody talked about Boeing; about how they had contracts backed up for years and years, about how they hired anybody they could lay their hands on. Talking that way they made Seattle shine like one of those huge old ships, all her white sails snapping with nothing but fair winds. I could hardly wait to climb onboard.

My first day in the city I found my way down to the ocean. A pile of people sleep in the parks near the water, but I slept right down by the ocean itself, because I'd never seen one before. I thought I wouldn't be able to see across the water, but there was land over there. I hoped maybe it was just islands. I'd never seen anything I couldn't see to the other side of, except the burned-up old plains back home. And they were just the world. I never expected to be able to see across that.

But I liked the noise of the swells hissing over the legs of the docks and the salty smell of the water. I took a big whiff, glancing around to make sure I was alone. Then I growled, "Avast you salty dog!" I don't even know what *avast* means, but that salt reminded me of all my old pirate books, of keel hauling and walking the plank and guys with hooks for hands and pegs for legs.

Turns out it wasn't the ocean. Was only Puget Sound. That's why I could see across it, because it wasn't really the Pacific, but just some crummy little sliver of it. Even so, I still liked the smell.

I got rousted early by cops and they told me I better sleep in the park. They were nice enough, like they could tell I was new here, though I tried to seem like an old hand. They said they were keeping people off the docks because a lot of tourists went there. Made sense to me really, and I shoved off.

I walked to the park, where most everybody was still asleep, some sprawled so wide open it was easy to see they were drunk as goats, or had been anyway, when they passed out. When they started to wake up, groaning and rubbing at themselves, like anybody'll do, I wished I was someplace where I couldn't see them. It's no good watching people wake up when you can see the day isn't bringing anything for them.

I wondered if this place might be the end of the plank, and I started walking south, where they said Boeing was. I put out a thumb, but it was harder getting rides here than back in Wyoming. A lot harder.

Took most of the day, but I finally got dropped off in a Boeing parking lot bigger than Chugwater. The factory or whatever looked bigger than Laramie. I whispered, "This is gonna be all right," and walked in and got pointed around to the hiring people.

I stood in front of this lady who sat behind her desk. She was a nice enough looking lady—somebody's mom in a business suit. She didn't hand me an application form but just looked at me in my jean jacket, frayed a little at the rolled-back cuffs, and at my cowboy hat, which was stained by everything in Chugwater. She asked what my degree was in—like the answer wasn't inked over every inch of my hayseed carcass.

When I didn't say anything she asked about my work experience. I'd never had a real job in my life. Just some pick-up work in the oil fields and some fencing and stuff out on the ranches. She sat waiting for an answer and I said I'd done a lot of different things and was a pretty quick learner. She smiled like you would at a puppy you knew you couldn't keep. She held out some forms for me.

I sat down and glanced through the papers. They were filled with questions I couldn't answer without ruining my chances. I tried for a while but finally for "last employment" I wrote, "Plundering the high seas." I smiled and glanced at the woman's nice, mom-looking face. I felt kind of bad for not having a chance and for ruining her forms, and I stopped smiling. But I scratched out my name and wrote in Edward Teach. It wouldn't hurt her or anything. She wouldn't know that was Blackbeard's real name. Not in a million years.

For no particular reason I wound up back down at the Sound that night. Funny how you spend a night someplace, on a bench even, and it gets to be a place to go back to. I walked by the park getting there and saw the same crowd, still panhandling some.

I was a little proud they didn't try to bum anything off me and I didn't feel too bad when I wound up by myself on the ends of the docks.

I curled up underneath my bench, using my pack for a pillow. Everybody slept on top of them, but I liked the idea of having those heavy planks over my body. It wasn't that I was worried so much, but there was an uneasy feeling about sleeping where all these strangers could see me. It was too naked-like. You see dogs do the same thing, curling up under a chair or table or whatever.

I could see through the slats of the bench, and I lay there looking at the night, pretending I was in a hammock belowdecks, the deck ringing with the footsteps of the night watch and creaking with the pitch and roll of the sea. But I hadn't even seen a real ocean yet, and I wound up thinking about Wyoming again, about being out camping someplace. I'd gone with my folks before, when I was little. I pretended I was doing that again, and that we were in bed early so we could get up at dawn and catch a mess of trout and grill them right over the flames for breakfast. You can char the skin that way and it'll peel right off, leaving you with just the hot, smoky taste of the meat. Here at the docks they sold all kinds of clams and mussels and other things I'd never even heard of, but I doubted any of it could touch trout cooked lazy that way.

I didn't know a thing about fishing in oceans or sounds, but all of a sudden I couldn't believe I hadn't brought my fishing rod. I'd never even been that crazy about fishing. It was just something we did when we used to go camping, so we could have those trout for breakfast. But I remembered us lying in our bags in the sagebrush, so many stars the night seemed white, and I really started to wonder how I could've forgotten that rod. I wondered how many other things I'd need that I might've left behind without knowing it.

I looked up through the bench slats. The lights from the city blotted the sky and I couldn't see a star anywhere, though I knew from the way the day'd been that the sky was clear. I wished I could've seen just one, just for a second. I'd never thought there was anything anybody could do to stars, and I felt pretty bad that I hadn't seen how easy it was just to block them out altogether.

I wondered what the old pirates would've done, if the stars they steered by just disappeared. I could see Edward Teach, legs spread wide, both gnarly hands white-knuckling the wheel, screaming bloody oaths at the sky and stars that had failed him. I could see how white his teeth would be in his black beard, the mast maybe glowing with Saint Elmo's fire, but I couldn't begin to see what he'd do without those stars.

Finally Blackbeard was shaking his cutlass at the sky and I couldn't sleep at all. It must've been around midnight, but I started wandering around, wondering what they would've used to steer by on black nights. I knew there had to be something, sextants or astrolabes or something, but I didn't know the secrets of any of that.

There were still quite a few people out and I liked that. Never see anybody out in Chugwater after ten or so. For some reason I called my folks—to let them know I was all right, I guess. They were sleepy, but they accepted the call and were glad to hear I was okay. I told them where I was and I told them you couldn't see the stars out here, but they didn't get it. My dad wanted to know if I was drunk. It was hard to tell if he was kidding or not.

Soon as I hung up I felt pretty stupid. You don't go around waking up people in the middle of the night to tell them you're all right. Not if you want them to believe you.

I walked around through the park again. The people who lived there were all pretty drunk by now. Two of them were fighting, the way drunks do, without much damage. It was warm out, but one of them was wearing a coat and I could hear it tear as they wrestled around. I walked back out to my dock.

Instead of getting under the bench I sat down on it and wondered what I'd try tomorrow. I had some money left, and I figured I might blow some of it on a motel. It'd be nice to get a shower.

I figured I'd head out of Seattle. People here said good stuff about places down the coast, in Oregon, or even California. I kind of wanted to stay by the ocean now. I still liked the smell of it; of the water and the other things in it I didn't know. Maybe I'd find a smaller place, some place that didn't bother outshining the stars.

I took a big breath of the ocean air and tried to compare all those smells with the lousy stink of sage. Sage's got a sharp smell, something you can't ignore. In Chugwater I'd always thought sage smelled like emptiness, like there's nothing there now and never will be.

I tried to remember that sage smell so I could hold it up against the ocean, but I couldn't do it. I knew what it had always reminded me of, but with the ocean all around me I couldn't remember the exact scent. Some of those things you think you'll never be able to forget, until you find they were only there because of all the other things they're tied to. Now I couldn't remember sage, though for the first time in my life I wanted to. I pictured the plant, the tiny silvery gray leaves and brittle branches, and I sniffed. But all I got was ocean.

There was a burst of noise from the park then—the lunatic yippings and laughings of coyotes. I started to smile and sat straight to hear them better. Coyotes'll hardly ever howl like you hear on TV. Maybe that's the way wolves sound, I don't know. Coyotes sound like they ought to be locked up in an asylum. They sound that crazy and wild. I always liked hearing them.

But I realized I was still on a park bench on the edge of what I'd once thought was the whole Pacific Ocean. I was in the biggest city I'd ever seen, one that blocked the stars, and I knew I wasn't hearing coyotes. I stood up and looked over the black water. I could pick out a shout here and there and laughing, and once a big run of happy swearing. It all came from the park, just right there on the edge of my ears. Really had sounded like coyotes for a second.

I slipped my pack on and headed out. I started south and walked all night. Got a ride after it got light, when I could see what I was getting into. I figured if there was light enough to see I might be able to tell when I reached a place that had a little of what I knew and a little of what I wanted. Salty and sagey all at once somehow. A place with pirates in cowboy hats, is what I thought, kidding around in my head. Big, black eye-patches, knives in their teeth, red bandannas around their necks, with—no, make that fencing pliers in their teeth. I laughed out loud. The guy driving asked what I was laughing about and I had to tell him, "Nothing."

I kept going, slow and in spurts, until I wound up in the top end of California. I found a beach there, in some kind of park, that had a sign on it about how Captain Drake, one of the greatest pirates of them all, had once pulled in here to fix his boat and had stayed awhile because of the protection the place offered. They called it Drake's Bay, and from there the ocean stretched out forever, just like it was supposed to. I'd sit and watch it sometimes, wondering about the places it went.

There were a lot of teeny little farms there, that they didn't call ranches, whether they ran cattle or sheep or whatever. I got a job fencing off and on, but steady enough from one farm to the next. After a while I even had an ad in the Yellow Pages, under "Fences." I was the Pirate Fencing Company, all by myself. A lot of times I could see the ocean right from where I was working. At night there were stars everywhere, except right down on the bottom edge of the sky, where San Francisco was.

I got myself an old beater of a truck and I got a place—rented, anyway—and I bought a fishing rod. When I called my parents this time I did it when I knew they'd be getting home from the oil fields, not in the middle of the night, and I didn't talk to them about the stars.

In fact I didn't talk to them much. I told them I was all right, and I knew they were glad to hear that, and they told me I ought to call more often. I wasn't sure if I could do that though. Just through the phone I could hear how the fields had beat them down another day, and how they didn't even know it themselves anymore. I could see their dirty faces, the lines all slacked out of them, like they'd been sleeping, though they were wide awake.

It seemed none of us could think of much to talk about, and when they said they should start getting their dinner together, out of the blue I asked if they'd been out camping at all, if they'd caught any of those little trout. They laughed at that, as if I'd asked them something funny—as if I'd asked if they were still saving my baby shoes or something. They said no, they hadn't done that in years and years. And when they said that I all of a sudden realized there were some things I was going to have to block out, things I'd have to go blind to on purpose. I wondered how I'd look with an eye patch, like the pirate in my phone-book ad. I told them I'd let them get to their dinner. They thanked me for that and I hung up, the reek of sage so thick I could hardly breathe.

I grabbed my fishing rod from beside the door and drove like a crazy person down to the ocean. I waded right out into Drake's Bay to make my cast. Instead of going back to shore and planting my pole, like I'd learned by watching the other surf cast-ers, I stayed out there. The waves came up to my thighs, almost knocking me down, then sucked back in behind me, trying to pull me out to sea. I thought about just letting them take over and I closed my unpatched eyes and took breath after breath of the salty air of that pirate bay.

Then I opened my eyes and looked out past the sparkling strand of my fishing line, past where anything could be seen. The day's clouds edged the horizon—pirate ships just heaving into sight. In the last ship in the line I could almost see Edward Teach leaning over the scuppers, smiling white in his dark face, shaking his cutlass to wave me aboard.

slipping

reared up against the bumper, freezing mud spattering my hands and, until I ducked, my face. Big, stiff clots of it thunked down on the roof of the station wagon, sitting there as I fought the spin of the tires.

When Robin glanced back, I grimaced, shaking my head. She let off the gas and smiled tightly, brushing the hair back from her face; her one nervous tic. I walked to her window.

We were barely off the road, but with the clouds coming lower and darker, and the wind picking up, the temperature dropping like a hammer, just the idea of getting stuck for good gave me a shiver. I said so.

Robin brushed her hair out of her face again and nodded toward the cooler. "At least we won't starve."

I smiled a little, wondering what she could have been thinking, packing enough for a whole family to spend a week out when all we were doing was taking a drive, escaping the echoing quiet of the house for a day, even if it was already practically the middle of winter.

"No," I said, "we shouldn't starve." I hunched my shoulders against the wind. "Freeze is more like it."

We didn't look at each other then, and I said, "Well, let's try rocking it a little. If that doesn't work I can cut some sticks. Stuff them under the tires. The way it's freezing, this mud is like grease."

But rocking it did work, and we were back on the road in a minute, Robin sliding across the seat for me to drive. Once I was in, Robin reached over and plucked a flattened drop of mud from my cheek. I rubbed at the spot, feeling the crinkle of dirt beneath my fingers. She kept looking at me, as if she was going to say something, and I looked back at her clean cheeks and nose, her bright eyes, wishing there was a trace of mud there I could lift off. Then she turned away, looking forward. "Ready?" she asked.

I took one more look as she pushed her hair away from her face and I remembered how she'd done that during my first visit to her house; the tumult of younger brothers and sisters tearing by us making kissing sounds as I tried to get her out the door. Our first date.

The night wrapped around us as we drove and sitting in the cramped silence I ignored the darts of snow flashing through the headlights—ignored the fact that we'd slid off the road once already. Even as the snow thickened into a blotting, frantic dance I barely slowed, ignoring everything but Robin saying nothing. Finally I blew out a long, loud breath. "This is getting ugly," I said.

She turned to look at me, then nodded, peering back into the storm. "Dad would call this a howler," she answered. She was always doing that: referring to her family, leaving me the siblingless outsider.

We drifted on through the slashing chaos of snow, only the tires making any sound at all. "I can't remember the last time we talked," I said at last, out with it.

She kept looking straight ahead. "I don't know anymore if you'll like what I have to say," she whispered.

"Try me," I countered, her words slicking me with fear.

For a moment she didn't move, then she raised her hand and rubbed at her forehead, drawing in a big, quivery breath. She brushed her hair back from her face. "It's happened, Jack," she said, the three words slipping out like a wish.

I listened to every one of her breaths.

"I sat beside you all day and couldn't figure out how to tell you. Packed that whole celebration feast."

The snow was everywhere. Whiteout. "What?" I said, though I knew what she must be saying.

"I'm pregnant, Jack." I turned to see her smile, the nervous tremble of it. "Don't ask me how."

"Robin!" I blurted, my stomach twisting with all the old fears. But I blurted "Robin!" again, and, "That's fantastic! How long? Are you sure?"

She watched me a moment before saying, "Of course I'm sure." She paused again, then whispered, "We're past the third month, Jack."

I cleared my throat. "Three months," I repeated. Longer than ever before.

She brushed her hair out of her face. Then she smiled. "I have the ultrasound pictures at home, Jack. You won't believe them."

"Three months," I said again.

"I wanted to be sure."

You can never be sure, I almost shouted, but made myself stop. Instead I stared at the snow before us, blinding bright in its instant in the light.

Barreling down the headlights' tunnel, I took a hand off the wheel to touch her, and said, "Robin, it's been so long I can't even remember the names we picked." It was a joke.

And that's when the car slipped. It straightened for an instant, with me doing nothing, just sitting behind the wheel. A bystander. Then we slid again, our rear end trying to swap with the front.

After what seemed a huge delay, I brought my hand back to the wheel, began fighting it, slashing the wheel one way, then the other. I heard Robin whistle in a breath, bracing.

We crunched into something near the back, which was where the front had been a second before, but the next impact was on the side and I felt Robin's hair whip against my face and I remember thinking, Get away! I can't see! though we were far past where seeing would do us any good.

I don't remember splashing in; just the headlights going out, leaving everything blacker than black. Then the sting of the cold, sharp as tongue-sharpened icicles. Water, I thought—we're in the river—though picturing Robin and her baby I'd never thought of how the highway strung along the river's path.

Then I heard Robin shout, "Jack! Jack!"

I was scrambling for the seat belt, but for an instant, a whole second maybe, I stopped short. There wasn't a better sound in the world than that shout; Robin needing to know I was all right, that I was with her.

Without a trace of light, the bubbling and rushing water surrounding us, soaking me, I said, "I'm fine, Robin."

"Jack!" she shouted back, banging at something, desperate beyond anything I'd ever heard.

"I think we're in the river," I said, too surprised and amazed to be scared yet.

She kept banging.

I reached out to touch her. "Try the window. Roll it down." For an instant I'd wondered if I was blind, or dead, and feeling the rough cloth of her coat made me nearly cry with relief. I let go and tried my belt again, but couldn't find the release anywhere.

"There!" Robin said, then, "No!"

"What?"

"We're floating."

My hands were underwater, as numb as the rest of me, but at last I found the button and slipped off the belt. "Get on the roof," I shouted. With her window open the river roared.

For some reason, instead of opening my own door or window, I followed Robin. I'd just felt my way to the opening when her boot slapped into my face, my nose, bringing stars to my eyes. "Are you on the roof?" I shouted.

"Yes," she yelled back. "Give me your hand."

Halfway through the window I reached into the blackness, feeling the touch of her fingers against my stiff, bricklike hand. I almost smiled, that we could find each other like that, that easily, even now. But before I could close my hand around hers, the car shuddered, lurching around sideways and shivering, twisting again, lining up with the current, but grinding against stone. Robin's hand no longer touched mine.

I slapped the rooftop, searching. "Robin!" I screamed.

I pulled myself up onto the slick metal of the roof. Water washed over it, but only inches deep. I pictured a big boulder in midstream, the bulge in the rushing flat of the water, the break of wave. I'm an island, I thought. A navigational hazard. "Robin!"

The car was still, grounded, and I got up on my knees, as if the blackness were a wall I could peek over. I cupped my hands around my mouth and screamed her name. Finally thinking, I turned downstream and shouted again. I waited, straining to hear over the rush of water splitting and boiling around me. I shouted again. And again. I listened to nothing but the answering roar of water, and wondered how she could have ever thought I wouldn't be happy to know.

At last, from somewhere below me, I heard a wavery cry, something unintelligible.

"Robin?" I shouted, as if it could be someone else.

"Jack!" she yelled. "Jack! Where are you?"

I didn't hear everything she said, mostly just my name. "On the car," I answered.

I didn't hear anything and I shouted, "Are you on shore?"

"I don't know." She sounded closer, louder somehow. Maybe a trick of wind.

"Are you on land?"

The car shifted and I dropped to my hands and knees, clawing as if my fingernails could grab into metal. I couldn't hear a thing over the pounding of my own heart, thudding as if it could keep us all alive.

When I eased up Robin was calling my name again. Frantic.

I didn't want to answer, wanted instead to go on hearing her call my name. "I'm on the car," I yelled.

What I heard was "I'm . . . trees . . . can't see." Or maybe it was, "I'm . . . please . . . our baby."

"Are you at the road?" I shouted.

The wind swirled whole sentences to me. "I don't know. Jack?"

I was shaking hard. She sounded like she was off to the left, but with the wind I wondered how much I could really tell. I fought to picture the road and the river, their joined paths. The road should be to the right. I looked that way uselessly.

"Robin? Are you on an island?" I shouted.

"I don't know."

"Are there boulders? Riprap?" If a car came along there'd be its lights. I thought as hard as I could. Maybe I could rescue her; a scene from old comic books.

"Where are we?" Robin shrieked.

"In the Snake," I yelled back, never having said anything so useless in my life.

"There's no boulders," she shouted a minute later. "I'm on the wrong side."

From there, even if a car did come, we'd be dead. No one was driving around tonight with their windows down. Nothing to hear. Nothing to see. Cold as it was, wet as we were, it wouldn't take long. "Robin?" I shouted. "I'm coming over."

"What?"

"Get ready," I yelled, standing to jump as far as I could, on my way back to her before I could think anything through.

"Jack!" she shouted, and I leapt at the word.

The water pulled instantly, and fighting against it I forgot how to do anything else, even breathe. I thrashed with my arms, lifting my head above waves I couldn't see. I couldn't feel if my legs kicked or not.

When the whole world was nothing but a tossing jumble of blackness and cold, twisting me until I had no idea which side of the river was which, even which was up, Robin's voice cut through again, my name sounding close enough to reach.

My knee struck something solid, then my hip. I rolled over and just as I remembered how to breathe I sucked in water. My hands hit, my shoulder. Gasping and spluttering, I rolled through the shallows, not able to think or move fast enough to get my arms and legs beneath me, to try and stand up.

Robin shouted again, sounding so close I thought I might be touching her. I wondered if this was what it was to die, hearing her coming closer and closer until finally, slipping underwater, I'd be able to reach her again.

I shouted "Robin?" not sure if the word came out. Then, out of the black tangle of air and water, she was clawing at my sleeve, at my collar, her face suddenly pressed against mine, her breath just like it had always been: the warmest thing I knew. Maybe this was what it was like to be born.

Robin didn't stop until she'd dragged me clear of the river. Then, clinging together for a few seconds, or minutes maybe, we didn't move, or say a thing.

I felt Robin's teeth chattering, her lips stuttering against my cheek. "Do you have matches?" she whispered.

"In my coat," I said, feeling heroic again for the instant it took to picture my coat in the back of the car, floating free. "No," I said.

"Jack. We have to get out of here."

I was sitting awkwardly, draped over a branch or log, maybe a rock. I shifted my weight, the tiny movement twisting every last bit of warmth away from my skin, bringing the freezing touch back instead, forcing out a gasp.

"If we stay here another minute we'll die," Robin said. "We have to get back to the road."

I could still feel her lips chattering against my cheek, her arms around me. "I don't know where the road is."

"Over there." She must have lifted her arm to point. The cold flooded in without it.

I tightened my grip around her, but the idea of sitting still with her held an attraction so strong I could sense death in it, and I forced myself up. Robin stood with me. Alone, I don't think I would've made it. We stood wobbly, hanging on to each other, my legs like stilts I'd never learned to use.

"Move," Robin said. "Walk in place. Run if you can."

I did as I was told, amazed to see her already the stronger one, the mother.

We shifted back and forth, still holding on to each other. If there was light enough to see, I guessed we'd look like marionettes, dangling from an amateur hand.

"Can you feel anything?"

"I'm not . . ."

Then Robin shouted something, too close to my ear to make out. She spun me round, letting go of me. Leaping to the side, she began jumping and waving, demented jumping jacks. It was a second before I realized I could see her, that there was light. She was signaling for help.

The car across the river was like a spaceship, a giant white beam splitting the night, snow rushing in a cone before it. Robin yelled and yelled, and though I knew I should too, I only stood beside her, watching her hopeless dance, reaching for the light as if it were a friend not seen in ages. I remembered how she used to reach for me that way, all the time, years before we'd given up saying the word *children*.

At the last second I thought to glance down at the river. In that final glimpse of light I saw flat water, not torn by waves or rock. It looked too wide to be true. And, as the car finished its slow turn through the curve, and Robin stopped jumping, I reached for her, the passing car dissolving into nothing more than two red dots, winking out.

Without hesitating, Robin said, "We have to cross the river."

"What if no other car comes?"

"Then we'll all die here." She took the hand I'd reached out, as if she could see it, and tugged me toward the water.

"Wait," I said, pulling back.

"We can't wait, Jack."

"Wading sticks," I said, thinking of that odd second of actually being able to see Robin, see her stretched out in her jumping jacks. Behind her the dead gray branches of the river brush reached into the air, angling up the way her arms did as she called out to the light.

I fumbled forward, groping for the branches, sweeping thumb-thick willow limbs every which way. They struck back like lashes. My hand touched something solid and I wrapped my arms around it, pushing it toward the ground until I felt the tingle in my numbed hands, the stinging crack shiver through the wood.

The stick was taller than I was and thick. I didn't look for another. "I can only find one," I said.

"Okay, let's go."

I stumbled to the sound of her voice, bumping into her. "We'll go together," I said. "I'll lean into the stick. You hang on to me."

"But if one of us falls . . ."

"We'll have a better chance together, Robin."

I felt her arms go around my waist, pulling us toward the water. "Please, Jack."

The shallows lasted so long I felt a flicker of hope. We must be almost across, I thought, both of us together. Leaning against my stick, the water pressing hard against me, but barely higher than my knees, I said, "Step," with every move, edging sideways, sliding my feet rather than lifting them, afraid I wouldn't be able to feel when they touched back down.

"You okay?" I asked, even talking a labor.

I felt her forehead touch between my shoulder blades in what must have been a nod. Her arms squeezed my waist so tightly I pretended that was all that made breathing so hard.

The next step was deeper, the water crawling up my legs, the pressure growing until I leaned at an impossible angle on my stick. The next was worse.

My legs were so deadened by the time the river pushed them from beneath me that I didn't know I was awash until my face hit the water. Robin was gone in the same instant, but the cold strangled my chest and I struck out in panic, letting go of my stick, of my hopes of making it across together.

Again I felt I'd been struggling forever, that I was reaching only for air, which was just as black as the water, when another spaceship came, the light blinding above me, too close to be real.

Rocks rimmed the night beneath the light; giant, jagged edges of black. I reached for them, then in the same movement felt myself knocking into them, bashing off and striking more downstream. I found a grip on a rock, and crawled onto it. Turning my head, I lay my cheek on the slippery, iced face of stone, listening to the rush of the water around me, feeling it tugging at my clothes, at my feet adrift at the end of my legs.

That's how I saw Robin, etched against the light like something Spielberg would do. She was waving again, a flat-footed jumping jack, and slowly I realized the light was not moving, was not sweeping past like the one before. Feeling the sharp edges of the rock beneath my cheek, I was so proud of her, making it on her own.

But faster than I could've guessed possible, there were people with lights, flashlights, clambering through the rocks, shouting my name. I thought answering would be brilliant, but I couldn't give up my hold on my rock, couldn't lift my head far enough or open my mouth wide enough to be heard. Truth was, I didn't want to move. I wanted to stay still so badly, wanted never to feel the cold touch I knew movement would bring, that I hoped their lights wouldn't reach me.

But even as I thought that, I squeezed my eyes tight against the glare of a light shone directly into them. I heard a voice shout, "Here!" and within seconds there was splashing beside me, a sucked-in run of swearing, and hands; hands pulling at me everywhere. I moaned, as loud a noise as I could make, trying to ask them to stop.

As they scraped and carried me to their car, I wanted to beg them to leave me alone. Then, remembering the moment the pressure of her hold was gone from my waist, I forced myself to whisper, "Robin?" I tried again, my voice a pitiful squawk.

"She's in the car already," said one of the pair of hands and we crested the bank, the flood of the headlights driving into my eyes like nails.

I twisted away from it as the hands set me down, began tugging at my clothes. Within seconds I was pushed into the front seat with Robin, a sleeping bag thrown over us, the heater blowing into the tube shaped from the bag. Robin hugged me, her entire body shaking against mine as her teeth and lips had chattered against my cheek. "Jack?" she whispered.

The car shifted through a U-turn, the driver swearing again, at the snow this time. There was a rush of talk about town and hospitals. Then, to somebody behind us, the driver said, "One of you strip down and crawl in with them. They're too cold to do each other any good."

And, as moments later a stranger crawled over the seat, a flash of white underwear bright for an instant before he slipped under the sleeping bag between us, crushing us, jamming me against the door away from Robin, I realized that I was naked as well; that Robin was naked, reaching over the stranger for me, saying, "Jack, are you there?"

"Of course," I answered, finding her hand and holding it against my face, her frozen fingers like so many sticks beneath my brittle touch. Suddenly I wished I could reach her belly, trace it for any signs of growth.

"Jack," Robin said. "Our baby?"

And the stranger, this naked person trying to save our lives with the warmth of his own body, blurted, "What? A baby? Aren't there just the two of you?"

chinook

There was a fog around Jessica at first, a fog of guys so thick I could barely see her. They thinned out soon enough, though, till she didn't have much of a reputation for friendly. But I knew most of those guys, and, if I was her, I wouldn't've been too friendly either. The rumors about her frostiness got around to hide their rejections.

She'd transferred to Montana State from Alabama State, but she wasn't Southern. Year before she'd been at Indiana, year before that Arizona. I knew all that. Even with the rumors people still talked about her. She wasn't your typical centerfold beautiful, but she had something striking hidden in her that turned heads, stopped talk about anything else.

The day I finally got up the guts to talk to her, March by now, she was in the student union, drinking coffee, filling out an application for the University of Alaska. I asked if I could sit down and she shrugged without looking up.

I said something like, "Alaska, huh? Where in the world are you from?"

She said, "I don't know."

I sat down anyway, saying, "I'm from Chinook."

She looked at me at last and I said, "It's named after a wind. You probably never heard of it."

She didn't answer and I explained, "It's pretty small. Fifteen hundred people. Fourteen ninety-nine now, I guess."

I laughed by myself and she set her pen down on her application and turned to really look at me. I was talking way too much.

"A chinook's a wind we get up there, out of the mountains. They say they only come in winter. It can go from ten below right up to fifty or sixty, all in an hour or two. Melts all the snow, floods the streets. After it blows through, though, the old temperatures come back, freezing everything all over again. But people love them. A breath of summer in the middle of winter."

I was babbling, but I couldn't quit. "My personal theory is that chinooks happen year-round. It's always windy up there, and if a chinook blew through in August, who could tell?"

"Who could tell?" she repeated, stopping me at last. But she gave me one of the smiles that'd made all those guys chase after her in the first place.

She was an Air Force kid, she told me, traveled all over the world, never staying more than a couple of years in any one place. Said the whole time she was growing up she couldn't wait to stay put, but when she was out on her own she kept on moving, even more than before. "Go figure," she said.

She was a junior, like me, but in her fifth year of school, because she lost credits every time she transferred. "Same as you lose something whenever you move," she said. I must have looked at her funny, because she added, "Books, pictures, underwear, you know."

And I said, "Yeah," like I knew. It wasn't a five-hour drive from Chinook to here. I said, "I've been to Canada once," but I said it dopey, as a joke. Chinook's forty miles from the border. Everybody's been to Canada.

She said Canada was the one place she'd never been. I told her where Chinook was and we laughed. I was going up next week to help with calving and I told her I'd take her to Canada if she wanted to go. She said she did.

She didn't go to Alaska that next year. She fell in love with the ranch and the wheat and the scrubby, battered windbreaks and, more gradually, with me. We'd go up to Chinook most weekends, and she was desperate to learn about everything. She helped with the calving and then with the branding and in the fall with the shipping. Once that was done and things slowed down she kept after me to teach her to hunt. I'd never been very excited about hunting, but I took her out for birds and we'd get some partridge and stuff. She said she'd never stopped like this before, never slowed down long enough to really see what was around her. She said she just couldn't get all that wind and sky under her skin fast enough. When she wasn't looking I smiled, seeing her face and hearing the way she'd talk about slowing down and not being able to go fast enough all in the same breath.

We'd see a lot of deer when we were out and she said she wanted to hunt those too. I like deer, like to watch them, but I shot one once and knew I never wanted to do it again. That's what cattle are for, and we always had enough of them frozen that there wasn't any excuse for shooting a deer. I told her that and she stared at me. Then she came across the grass and hugged me and kissed me once. She said, "I really am getting the best of it. Of everything."

I couldn't agree with that out loud, even though I wanted to. I said, "This must all seem pretty hick to you."

What she said was, "Let's get married."

I managed to say, "When," and she said, "Whenever," which was vague enough I thought she might have been thinking out loud more than meaning anything. We'd known each other for eight months then.

But we did get married that June, a week after school was out, and we took over one of the houses out on the ranch. I started working in town at the elevator and Jess took a job at the store, so we could ride into work together. But she quit the store after a while and started working with my folks and my sister, running the ranch.

We were all over each other, you know, like newlyweds'll be. She'd come in with shit all over her boots and grass seed blown into that pile of sunny brown hair and I'd look at her and couldn't believe this had actually happened to me. I'd always wanted to get off the ranch and into town, even if it was only Chinook. I'd had enough of cow shit and wind. But seeing her like that was enough to keep me anyplace.

She'd undress like it was nothing, which always kind of amazed me too. How she could figure she was nothing, no matter what she was doing, was beyond me. I'd lose track of what she was saying sometimes, all lost just staring at her. Once she got so wound-up about something she started making dinner and getting ready for a shower at the same time. Finally she found herself standing at the stove in her underwear and she hit herself on the forehead, saying, "Shower, Jess. That's what you were doing." Then she pranced out of sight to the bathroom.

When I heard her shower start up I looked through the kitchen window, up to the big house, realizing I couldn't even picture what went on up there anymore. Everything I knew or wanted was here now, and I felt vaguely sorry for the rest of them, because they'd never know anything this good.

The baby came the next year, a girl, and I wanted to name her Jessica, because I couldn't think of any girl I loved being called anything else. But Jessica wouldn't have any of that junior stuff and we settled on Katrina. Well, she settled on it anyway. I thought it made her sound like a foreigner; a Russian or a Hutterite or something. But pretty soon she was just Katy anyway, though Jess always took the time to call her Katrina.

Jess spent less time with the ranch then and more time at home. She put stencils around the walls in Katy's room and built some shelves and sewed teddy bears and stuff like that. I hadn't known she could do any of that kind of thing and she said she hadn't either. "But," she said, "I guess you can do anything if you think you have to."

I sat down beside her on the bed, the sag of the mattress pushing our shoulders together. I put my arm around her. I was twenty-four then and the guy who'd run the elevator had just had a heart attack and retired, leaving me in charge. I'd been doing that for a few weeks and was past the stress part. I thought I'd learned the same thing Jess had—that you can do anything you have to.

I wound up locking those moments into my mind, stunned by my own happiness, and even when things began to change I still had those pictures. Regardless of what was going on around me I held them up, evidence of how happy we were. I used those pictures as blinders, though of course I didn't realize that until later—until after the pictures had been lost in the move, just like Jess said was bound to happen.

After Jess quit working the ranch I'd sometimes catch her standing at the window for long stretches, holding Katy, the two of them looking out over the fields, toward the rough breaks of the bluff. I'd wonder what she was looking at, since nothing out there ever changed, but it seemed like she was thinking about things and I was afraid to disturb her.

Once Katy could walk well enough through the grass and the gopher holes they took long walks together. Jess hadn't been hunting since she'd had Katy, but she'd come back and tell me of the places they'd been, places I recognized as places I'd shown her when she'd just come up to this country. I wondered why she'd keep going there, but she'd come home breathless, her hair full of seeds and her face aglow, and she'd tell me about all the things they'd seen. Sometimes she asked if I remembered certain times we'd been places together and of course I'd say I did. Seeing her excited again was enough to convince me that everything was as good as it had always been, and I wasn't about to say I might have forgotten a detail here or there.

This went on until the night of my twenty-seventh birthday. Things like birthdays and holidays always swept Jess away. She was constantly decorating the house for the seasons: putting up balloons and banners and things like that. During the holidays my folks and sister used to spend more time at our house than up at the big house, which was the same as it was every other day of the year. I was prouder about that than I realized. And I was counting on all her preparation to cheer her up some, to bring that smile back from wherever it'd gone.

A bunch of the guys in town took me out for a drink after work and though I wasn't really that fired-up about it, I thought I'd keep it quick and get on home. The bartender made a big deal about the birthday, buying a free round, and the guys I was with had to get me a round of their own, and then another, and when I finally called it quits I took a lot of ribbing. Everybody knew Jess, who only got more of that haunting beauty each year. It was something she couldn't help, and I don't think she'd've looked like that if she had a choice. She didn't much like people noticing her. But her cheeks stood out more and more, still looking smooth and soft all the same. Her skin did that, smooth enough to glow, and seeming to grow brighter by the year, as if something was alight inside her. People couldn't help but notice her. So I got ribbed about running home to my birthday treat.

They'd planned a night of it though and we had ourselves a driver. We all piled into a four-door truck and started for the ranch.

I had to leave my car in town, but they said this was part of my present, getting chauffeured around.

When we got to the place on the highway where you can't see town anymore, but you can just make out the ranch—some fence lines and the jutting row of cottonwoods that make up the windbreak for our house—we saw a car sitting on the side of the road, puffing out wreaths of white exhaust, as if the engine was catching its breath.

It was an odd spot to stop and we pulled over and our driver asked if they needed help. Then everyone was laughing and I looked over and saw it was Jess and that the car was our car. I felt kind of foolish, not recognizing it right away. From where I sat I could just see the edge of the car seat and Katy's leg bouncing up and down. I could imagine the tune she was humming, the same one she'd been going over this morning when I'd left for work. She could get a tune stuck in her head and go on with it until you thought you'd scream.

The truck I was in pulled out then and I asked what was going on. I hadn't been able to see Jess's face, just her chest and lap, and her hands, fidgeting on the steering wheel. They were all laughing then, about me rushing to my birthday treat and my treat rushing in the opposite direction. I twisted around backward, watching the exhaust thin out and disappear as the car warmed up. Then we turned onto the dirt and I couldn't see her anymore. "What was she doing?" I asked.

"Said she'd forgotten something she needed," the driver told me.

"She was all right?"

"Sure she was all right. Think we'd just leave her?"

That got some more laughs and I figured she must have pulled over to search for her shopping list or something. She could get awful scatterbrained if something was on her mind. Must've forgotten the balloons, I remember thinking.

They dropped me off at the house with more hooting, then roared off honking, screaming the happy-birthday song at the top of their lungs.

I stood in the driveway, thinking of Jess making the last-minute run to town for balloons and I smiled thinking that all those guys knew how I felt about her, and that they thought enough about Jess to envy me being with her. At least enough to tease me about it. They'd all been married as long as I had, some longer, and they seemed tired of each other. Nobody made jokes about any of them with their wives. Some of them were already divorced and some of them, it was common knowledge in a town the size of Chinook, were already having affairs.

I was still smiling, but Jess's hands, fiddling with the steering wheel, were hard for me to shake. They had that same anxious look that seemed to burn brighter and brighter in Jess, like she was just barely able to keep something inside from bursting into flame. More feverish than excited. It was the look I'd soon realize I was hiding behind my pictures of the happy times, and I wondered what that was all about. But I walked up onto the porch and nearly went inside before I stopped myself.

No matter that she did it every year, Jess always expected me to be surprised by her decorations. And in a way I was, surprised that she could be like that, that she'd take so much time for a bumpkin from Chinook. So I sat down on the porch swing, where we watched the thunderheads roll in from the plains in summer and I waited for her, not wanting to go inside until she said it was all right.

But it was fall again, late fall, heading on into another winter, and I just had my work shirt on and pretty soon I got cold. She should've been back by now, and I walked down the gravel drive, to see if I could see her returning. The wind moaned through the cottonwoods, cold from Canada, and I thought I'd just sneak inside and grab a coat. There was no way she'd know I'd ever been inside.

I ran back to the house, trying to chase away the chill that way, and banged through the door into the living room. I hunched over the radiator for just a second before getting my coat, because I knew she'd be home any second. Then I realized what I'd seen. I turned around and looked at my house and it was just the same as it had been when I left it that morning. There wasn't any preparation for any kind of celebration at all.

I got my coat and put it on, unable to shake the chill, even inside, and I walked around the house. Nothing. Not a crepe-paper streamer or a cake or a single thing. I was embarrassed by how disappointed I was and the very first of those pictures I'd been hiding behind slipped away.

I went outside and sat back down on the porch swing, huddled deep in my coat. There was one of those faceless gray fronts easing in from the north, as if hoping no one would notice. Not a cloud line so much as a hazy wave of darkness on the edge of things, that really can sneak up on you without you seeing it. The wind was picking up in front of it though, giving the storm away by its keening through the bare, black branches of the cottonwoods.

I shivered inside my coat and waited until it was nearly dark. I wasn't waiting so much, but just sitting there stunned, watching all those pretty, happy pictures falling away, revealing, too late of course, the way Jess had looked after her long, lonely walks. The chill flushed her cheeks, but even so there was that light underneath, showing the banked fire there, about to burst back into flame. It'd been there all along for me to see.

It was dusk when my parents' truck pulled down the road and up the drive. I could see the big house from where I sat and I'd heard the engine of the truck start up and I'd seen the lights come on and I'd listened to it crunch the hard-packed gravel. Time was they would have walked, but not anymore, not with Dad's hips.

They were coming down for the party. Coming just to see Jess's face lit up with excitement the way it'd get times like these. I knew the dark house behind me would create a big question mark before they even got out of the car. I listened to the doors slam and I heard my sister say, "Maybe they're in town."

"Naw, she always has the party here." That was my dad. I was shocked to hear him add, "Maybe she's just giving him his present a little early." He laughed. "We'll have to knock."

Mom said something like, "Hush yourself," giggling too, and they were all on the porch before they made me out in the dying light.

They stopped then and no one said anything. Seeing me out there alone in the dark put it beyond something they could joke past. Finally Dad said, "Where's Jessica?"

I said, "I don't know."

"What do you mean you don't know?"

When I didn't answer my father hooked the storm door open with his cane and marched into my house, flicking on lights. He hates unknowns. Mom hesitated, then followed. My sister sat down next to me in the porch swing.

"What in the world, Terry?"

"I've got this feeling" was all I said.

She patted her hand on my thigh, which was something Jess had always done. Neither Jess nor I were great talkers, and sometimes, if something was bothering one of us, we'd wind up just touching like that, rather than working it through in words. I wondered now if that was part of what was going on right now.

Then my dad shouted out from the back of the house, the bedroom, "There's a note here." He sounded victorious, as if it had been a treasure hunt.

My sister jumped up and ran for the back of the house. "I'll get him before he reads it," she whispered.

A minute later they all came marching out together, slow and dirge-like. My sister eased that note down onto my lap, like if she'd've dropped it the weight might have broken my bones.

They just kept right on walking, back into the truck, and Mom said, "Come on up to the big house, Terry. We'll all be there."

I flattened that note against my thigh, to keep the wind from taking it away, and I sat there knowing they'd read enough to tell me what it said by the way they'd trooped out of here. I listened to the bang of the car doors up at the big house. With a wind gust I even heard the screech of the storm door, then its slam.

I stayed out until that sneaky, darkling storm blotted out every little bit of light, even making the yard light at the big house quaver and dim. It started to snow and I went on inside, where my dad had left on all the lights.

I sat down at the kitchen table, an antiquey kind of thing Jess had bought in Great Falls. It was round with great lion paws for feet. Oak probably, and it had once given me a gigantic sliver. I spread the note on it and saw that there was no *Dear anybody* starting it and I could have just about told you what it said without reading it.

It said: "I started to decorate this morning, but I just couldn't face it. This is a terrible thing to do to you on your birthday. I thought I was miserable here the last year or more, but knowing how this is going to hurt you is really showing me what miserable is. I can't stay to change that though. My settling-down experiment has failed.

"I always told you I lost something every time I moved, but I didn't even know myself that part of what was lost was inside. I just used this place up, Terry. There's nothing I can do about that. I have to get to something new or I will lose my mind. All the sky, and the wind that never stops, used to be so magic. Now they seem like something I'm disappearing into, being worn-down by, same as the hills. I've got to leave before there is nothing left of me.

"You are what I'm losing this time, and I'm sorrier than sorry about this, and about you. You're the goodest person I know."

That was it. Not even signed. But it had so much of Jess in it I about gave out. *Goodest.* I could see her working over that before she put it down. Best was the right word, but it wouldn't mean enough; best at what? Good was what she meant, that I was a good person. The best at being good. Wasn't much consolation.

I sat in my little house and suddenly one of Katy's endless tunes snuck into my head. I tried to lose it before it could take hold, panicky that it would repeat within me forever, but the only other sound was the wind, rattling the windowpanes and scraping the cottonwood branches together. I finally thought of Jess locked up here, day after day, talking baby talk to Katy and listening to the wind. I was amazed she'd been able to put that note into paragraphs. If it'd been me it would've poured out so hard I doubt I'd've remembered periods.

I walked to the front door and stepped outside. The snow was really coming down, though with the wind I couldn't tell if it was just ground snow blowing, or something that'd really amount to something. I tried to remember if I'd put the snow tires on Jess's wagon. I pulled up my collar and walked through the stinging snow, up to the big house and into the tractor barn. The snow tires were gone and I was glad I had done that much for her. I walked back down to my place and turned off all the lights. Then I turned the porch light back on, just in case. But I knew there wasn't going to be anyone drawn back to that little dot of cold light.

I walked around my darkened house, eventually drawn back to the porch light myself. Through the glass the snow made hard white flashes in the glare. I glanced to the big house, bathed by the yard light but dimmed all the same by the rush of snow, blurred down to the edges.

I felt like moving out onto the porch—sitting down again in the swing, as if by waiting longer she might come back. But that would've been hiding again, behind pictures that hadn't existed in years.

I sat down on the love seat in the living room and wondered where she would've headed. She had the whole world to pick from, and all I knew was this one corner of nowhere. She'd once told me that's why she loved me.

I saw why that wore out. She'd seen everything in the world but, for a while, she'd thought that I'd seen more, that I'd seen the finer things she'd always rushed past. So she slowed down, thinking it was something she could just choose to do. And maybe she could've. She was awful strong. But she slowed down enough to learn about me too.

Sure, I knew where the partridge were likely to blow out of the grass, and I knew what kind of weather different clouds were bringing in, and I knew I didn't like to kill deer, but she'd figured that all added up to something—an inner vision or something. When she found that I really hadn't seen any of this—that she could live with me and have me see not one thing about her desperation— it must have been the biggest disappointment in the world. Like it'd been for Katy when she decided Santa Claus was something I'd personally made up.

All of a sudden I saw Jess and me sitting on our nappy white bedspread, our shoulders and arms touching down to the elbow. She was holding Katrina, brushing some of her wispy black hair away from her eyes, and looking at me, with the smile that probably still haunts some business-school graduates. Even then I'd seen it falling apart, but just looking at Jess's smile made me afraid there'd be a day I couldn't see it anymore. So I hid behind the good times and hoped they would last forever. Who wouldn't have?

I stood up then and turned on the lights. I turned them all on. I couldn't stand the darkness. I dragged an old box into the living room and started to wonder what I should pack. I didn't have a clue where I might be headed, but I had an idea Jess'd had no clearer picture. I was guessing Canada, because ever since we'd first met that'd been a joke—Canada, the one world the world traveler had never seen. I thought it might be the place I'd find her.

First thing I put in that box was that old, nappy bedspread, for padding, then I put in all the pictures I had of Jess, and Jess and me, and Jess and me and Katrina. I folded the ends of the spread over the top of the pictures, then put a pillow on top of that, for added protection.

I wandered around the house after that, not at all sure of what else I wanted to take. I put some clothes in and packed the box into the bed of a ranch truck. I felt bad, leaving all those pictures out there in the snow, but I knew well enough that I could never put those blinders back on, though I missed the idea of them already. I wondered if I somehow managed to find Jess what kind of nicks and bruises we'd get without hiding behind any old times. They were bound to make the final picture something not quite as glossy as the first ones.

I started the truck, sitting a minute to let it warm up. The snow shot through the headlights like tracers. I was scared, you know, about what that final picture would look like. But, at the same time, I was excited about trying to find Jess and make it all up to her. Whether I found her or not, I couldn't bear the thought of being left behind in the calm, quiet, cold that follows every chinook, and I backed out of the driveway and started off.

the fairest
OF THEM ALL

I hadn't heard the float plane and suddenly Jean stood outside my door in a dark, tailored suit, deep red hair falling all down her shoulders—someone you'd expect to see walking into a skyscraper. She had to step back so I could swing open the storm door. Just that tiny retreat made me smile, then wince. I'd never seen her back away from anything. Once the door was out of our way I gave the float plane a wave, letting the pilot know we were all right. As he taxied off across the lake Jean and I stepped together, half in the house, half out.

She said, "How've you been, stranger?" at the same moment I did. Then she took a big, shaky breath and looked around. "This is some hovel, Bro'," she said. "Exactly what I expected."

I shrugged and smiled back. "It's small, but it's dirty."

"The roof leaks, but the windows are broken?"

"Yeah, like that." We stood there smiling at each other, never so awkward in our lives, until Jean said, "Mind if I come in?"

We laughed a little but as I hung up her coat, when I wasn't looking at her, I said, "So how are you? Really?"

"I'm fine, Jim. Twins are supposed to know that about each other. Has it been so long we've lost our ESP?"

"Not even ESPs can make it that kind of distance. Not through L.A. smog."

She smiled at that too, even laughing about what she'd gone through to reach Alaska in one day. "Planes are supposed to have stewardesses, Jim," she said, "and big jet engines. And they're supposed to land on runways, not lakes."

Her smile faded and she sat down on the soft couch, sinking deep. She sighed. "I'm sorry, Jim. I was a little freaked-out on the phone. I didn't mean to worry you. It just got so fucked there at the end."

"Do you want I should have a word wit' him?" I said, talking Mafia, touching the shotgun I'd been cleaning while I waited for her.

She still managed to keep a smile and I thought maybe she really had been just blowing off steam when she'd called, crying and begging me to take her in. She'd never had to beg for that. Not from me.

She brushed her hair away from her face. "I couldn't believe the judge," she said, as if she'd been asked to explain. "Who ever heard of the husband winning child custody?"

"Goddamn Californians," I said, a whisper of an old joke.

"No kidding," she sighed, and just when I was afraid she might cry she stood up and said, "But don't give me any shit about L.A. smog. At least they've got heat down there."

Still in her expensive courtroom suit, Jean bent down to the wood stove and started carefully building a fire, layering the kindling in so it couldn't help but burn. She surrounded the kindling with bigger sticks, Lincoln-Log fashion, building a little home to burn down. I watched, tempted to tell her not to get herself dirty. Instead, when the flames had taken root in the walls, I walked into the kitchen and mixed a couple of drinks.

We stayed up late, dodging around the custody fight, Jean only dusting off the barest bones of the court battle. She talked more of L.A. and her modeling work. She'd quit that a few years back to have the kids, but she talked now as if that had never happened.

I figured whatever she wanted to talk about was her business, and she asked most of the questions. She wanted to know how my guiding had been going and I told her how it had taken off in the last few years. I mentioned the names of a few Hollywood types I'd taken out, people I thought she might know. She laughed hysterically, saying things like, "That asshole?" or, "That bitch can't fish, can she?"

When she asked about it, I told her, "No, I never told any of them you were my sister."

She stared at me a moment, but she sounded more tired than mad when she said, "It's nothing to be embarrassed about, Jim."

"Embarrassed?" I said. "Who said anything about embarrassed? It would have been tooting my own horn. I was never any good at that." She didn't look very convinced. "Besides," I said, "it would've been bad business, letting those women know my sister was the Fairest of Them All." That was something she used to ask when we were kids: "Jim, Jim, handsome and tall, who is the fairest of them all?" She knew there was only one possible answer.

She asked about my love life and kidded me about my lack of girlfriends, saying how they'd be after me down in L.A.; me being the strong, silent, mountain-man type. She said everything there depended on type. Type was critical.

She asked why I wasn't taking any babes out fishing. "Those Hemingway girls maybe," she suggested. "They're into this outdoor stuff, aren't they?"

It was an old joke, Jean trying hard to be her old self, but with Margaux's suicide and Mariel fading away, I could tell she wasn't thinking of anything yet. Still I managed to say that they'd just left, both of them, and those had been a wild few nights. I said I'd had to kick them out early, telling them I had an even hotter one on the way. She got serious then and said she hoped she hadn't screwed anything up by coming on no notice. I told her not to be stupid and tried to be more careful of what I said.

Even though we'd made it a late night I couldn't sleep and I was up early. I built a fire and stood in the kitchen, looking at the day growing strong outside the window. The firs swayed in a wind I should've seen was bringing in weather and I sipped coffee I'd made too strong because I wasn't paying attention to that either. She snuck up on me, surprising me when she said, "Thanks for the fire."

I could tell by her morning voice that she was surprised and pleased I would've thought of her. She'd always been that way in the mornings.

"I know how you city-girls are," I said, turning away from the window. She crossed the room, flushed from the shower, dressed sloppily in one of my union suits. "Got to love that lingerie," I said, but even through the loose red cloth I could see her breasts sway as she poured herself a cup of coffee and dropped into a chair at the table. I turned away and said, "It really has been too long."

"I know. My fault."

"Maybe you better chill out on the sexy stuff for a while," I said, wagging my finger at the union suit. "Till I can remember you're my sister."

She laughed and cupped one of her breasts through the cloth, bouncing it up and down. "These saggy old things would drive anyone to distraction, I know." She was quiet a second. Maybe I blushed. "Jesus, Jim. You've got to get out more often."

She let go of herself. "Milker tits," she said, suddenly angry. "You don't know what kids do to you."

I couldn't think of anything to say after that and we sat in the quiet while the day grew to full light. Jean took a sip of her coffee and winced.

"I screwed it up," I said.

"Still thinking about those Hemingway girls I bet."

"That's it," I said, though for a moment I couldn't remember what she was talking about. There was another long silence after that, as if we'd both forgotten how to talk.

Jean broke the quiet, asking, "What would you be doing if I wasn't here?"

I shrugged. "Nothing in particular."

"Standing staring out the window?"

"Probably. If I'd stayed up drinking till two."

"Still can't sleep late?"

I shook my head and turned to pour a little water into my coffee. It really was terrible. She held her cup out for some too. "Were you going hunting?"

"I guess so. Try to get at least one trip into the ponds before they freeze."

"Mind taking me?"

I stared at her. "You really want to?"

"I haven't shot in years. Or paddled." She tried her coffee again, wincing even with the water. "I think I'd love to."

"I've still got your gun," I told her.

She looked so surprised I had to say something. "Mariel likes to use it when she's up," I said. "Or maybe it was Margaux. I could never tell them apart. Hell, I can't even pronounce their names."

On the river Jean held her old shotgun across her thighs, like we used to as kids, and I crept the boat around the inside of all the river's bends and bays and backwaters, hoping to surprise anything that might be resting there. Time after time there was nothing and she'd let out a long sigh, putting her gun back in her lap and taking up her paddle again. I told her the ducks would all be on the ponds, but she'd never been in Alaska and she thought everyplace was like the marsh country in Wisconsin, where we'd grown up. At least that's how she wanted things to be now.

Looking at her in the bow of my canoe, at the turned-back sleeves of my wool shirts, and the little-kid-looking rolled-up cuffs on my wool pants, I wondered if there was anything else I could've given her. She'd come all the way to Alaska with nothing but the courtroom suit she'd been wearing.

By mid-afternoon we hadn't seen a duck and we weren't being careful going around the corners anymore. I didn't talk at all, except to answer her rare questions about the river and the ponds and such. I knew she hadn't come all the way up here to hunt. She wanted to talk about all of it, about the things she'd been screaming and crying about on the phone that night. So I waited, paddling when I had to, my ears straining a little, in case something might start leaking out of her proud, broken world.

We hadn't made a sound but a teal suddenly broke out of a side channel, three or four feet off the water, straight away from us in our canoe. Jean changed her paddle for her gun and I hunched down, bracing.

The blast emptied into the lowering gray sky, sounding small and hardly lethal in all that open, and she followed through for a second, but the quick herky-jerky flight of the teal never slowed.

Jean lowered her shotgun and swore. I said something about taking it easy. She hadn't shot in years and years. A hit would've been a miracle, I said, not that miss.

She told me to go to hell. She insisted, through clenched teeth, that she was the lucky one. She said she'd always been the lucky one and that she was good at this. "Better than you," she added, glaring over her shoulder before turning back to the river and empty sky. She had been a better shot when we were kids, but that was a long time ago.

Jean didn't pick up her paddle and I stared at her stiff back, at her wide shoulders, and instead of thinking about her temper I remembered when she'd first started lifting weights. I'd found her on my bench, doing presses with just the bar. This was in high school and her looks were already otherworldly. I was the envy of every boy in class, though I'd always ask what could be more use-less than a *sister* who looked like that. She glistened with sweat and between breaths she said, "The Mae West look is out, Bro'. They go for muscles now. Muscles and boobs." She'd always talked like that with me. And she'd always known exactly what she was going to do in her life.

Jean still wasn't paddling and the river twisted through a nest of weathered snags, splitting the water like broken, gray teeth. I steered through them, coming close to a few without her helping from the front. The water curled around the branches and fell away grumbling.

When I edged the canoe into the bank just downstream Jean sat still for a moment and I waited for her to move. "Are these the ponds?" she asked without looking at me.

"Not two hundred yards away. Right through the willow."

"Want me to get out?"

"No, I want you to sit there on that gorgeous ass all day while I hold the boat."

Then she laughed, too loud really for as close as the ducks were, but it was a pretty sound in the cold air. I stepped out of the canoe and held it while she got out. The sand was stiff but not quite frozen hard. "I hope they're still open," I said, wondering about ice.

As we reached the willows pinpoint flakes of snow began to sift around us. I touched Jean on the shoulder and pointed. "Bet you haven't seen that in a while."

"Oh, we go to Aspen every winter." She turned to me and lifted her eyebrows. It was the first slip she'd made. "I've kept in touch with the snow," she said. "And the cold, of course. There's always been that."

A few of the flakes touched her head and stuck without melting. They weren't white then so much as icy blue, with all that dark hair behind them. Though she was a fair letter writer, I hadn't seen Jean for nearly six years, except on magazines now and then. And there hadn't been many of those in the last few years. I'd almost forgotten how pretty she really was, not just the way the photographers fake everything.

She smiled at me and asked what I was staring at.

"I was trying to remember if I'd ever seen you without make-up."

"Enough to wake the dead isn't it?"

"Jeff Seymour would die to be here right now."

"Jeff Seymour?" she asked, then remembered. "Jeff Seymour! My god, how can you remember people like that? I haven't thought of him in years. Since high school!"

"I bet he hasn't stopped thinking of you."

"Poor Jeff," Jean said.

"He had a case of the Jeans for sure."

"Poor Jeff," she said again. "What a nut case he was."

We stood there and I saw Jean smiling, absentmindedly peeling a small strip of bark from a frozen willow. When she caught me watching she said, "Ready to show me your ponds?"

We followed a moose path into the willows, the dead leaves thick on the ground and loud underneath our feet. The snow kept up its slow, steady drift and I was surprised how low and heavy the clouds were. They'd snuck up on me like they never had before.

As we neared the pond Jean smiled at the racket coming from the water. We sat a second and I asked Jean how many she could still tell by their voices. She knew the mallard right off, and could tell the widgeon, but couldn't remember the name. When I said it she slapped herself on the forehead. There was a sudden rip of honking, the deep bark of the male, answered immediately by the higher call of a female. Jean leaned in to me and whispered, "When I can't tell a goose anymore bury me out on the back forty."

I took Jean to the head of an old beaver run cutting like a trench to the water's edge. I told her if she'd crawl down till she hit water she'd be breathing down their necks. I told her I'd go around the pond so we'd have them between us and that I'd stand up first. They'd all be going her way then. "You'll have more shooting than you'll know what to do with," I said.

She kept nodding, without saying a word, as if she couldn't wait for me to leave her there alone.

I went wide, keeping the willows between me and the pond, and I was able to jog a little. It helped me warm up after sitting in the canoe. I slowed when I turned back to the pond and soon I was on my hands and knees, and finally on my belly, slithering through the tall, dead grass, watching the grounded flakes melt when they touched my bare hands.

I'd always hunted this spot alone, from the beaver run where I'd left Jean. Most guides will hold back a place or two for themselves, something safe from the clients. I'd never come in from this side though, and it looked like an entirely different world. I wondered if I could do that to other places I knew, try them from some different direction and have them become new again. It would be like discovering untouched continents. I wondered if I'd ever be able to look at Jean that way, seeing her in some way I'd missed before.

The grass led all the way to the bank and I couldn't have gotten closer if I was invisible. I lay still, peering through the dead gold bars of the grass at the covered surface of the water.

There were a few hundred ducks milling about in front of me, anxious with the change in weather. Widgeon, pintail, mallard, teal, scaup, goldeneye—just about everything. But on the other side, between shore and the abandoned beaver lodge, a ribbon of geese strung across the water. There were even some onshore, not ten yards from where Jean lay hidden in her trench.

I gathered my knees under me so I could go up all at once and I stood.

There was a moment, a quick second maybe, when the pond just went still. The ducks made a few weak paddles, turning to me, as if they couldn't believe I was anything but an apparition, some trick of snow. Every goose's head came up at once, like periscopes, their necks stretched to the limit. Dumbfounded.

Then the stillness was over, the honking and flapping of the geese like an explosion. The ducks were everywhere, the puddlers leaping straight up and the divers running across the water, building takeoff speed. I picked out a pintail drake, because I wanted to show it to Jean, and I pulled the trigger. They were so close and tightly packed that the drake fell, as did two birds behind him. On my second shot a mallard fell alone.

The ducks were confused, circling the pond, offering shot after shot. I reloaded and glanced across the pond, realizing I hadn't heard Jean shoot. I saw her, blurred a little by the snow, standing still, holding her gun at her side. The geese were already in a solid group, flying south over the river, long out of range.

I watched her standing alone, making no attempt at the ducks winging over her and instead of shouldering my gun again I turned my back to the pond and retraced my steps, circling back to my sister.

The snow was coming down a little harder by the time I reached her. She was standing at the end of the beaver run, the pond empty and still now, silent before her. Only the dead ones drifted on its surface, blowing our way with the wind that carried the snow. Jean wasn't crying but there were traces of the last of her tears across the planes of her cheeks. I whispered, "Jean?"

She shook her head and turned away, hiding her face. "All those geese," she said.

I touched her shoulder and she leaned into my hand until I was holding her up. "I was so sure I was ready to be a mother," she said.

"You are a mother, Jean. The courts can't change that."

"Just carrying them doesn't make a mother, Jim. You couldn't know a thing about it."

"Tell me."

"I don't know if there's anything left to tell."

She dropped her head against my shoulder, both of us still looking toward the pond, the snow thick now, dimpling the water. While Jean tried to talk I watched the dead ducks edge over to us, still a long way off.

"He had videos, Jim. At the trial. I never even knew about them."

For a second there was a flash, the barest violent outline of Jean with her small children, colored red, like her temper. I closed my eyes and whispered, "What kind of videos?"

"Oh, the usual," she said, so casually I winced. "When it fell apart, I kind of did too. I would have gone with anybody if I thought they really liked me. Would have? Not would have. Did. He had people watching me, filming it."

I hugged her a little tighter, ashamed for what I'd been able to picture.

"They made quite the splash, believe me. That famous body naked with all those men. My lawyer tried to get them blocked as inflammatory. But I think they all wanted to see them pretty badly. I left the courthouse. It was all over after that. What kind of a mother would a raving slut like that make? What kind?"

"You're no slut, Jean," I said.

"Oh, I think I am, sometimes."

"Then you're wrong."

"Yes, something is wrong. I wanted to be a mother. I really needed to do that." She took a deep breath that quivered. "The modeling was about over, Jim. We're getting old. That's the worst type to be. I'd decided it was time to be a mother. That was my next step. I'd decided.

"Now what the hell am I going to do?"

I didn't have any idea. I stood in the snow and she let me hold her a little while. Then she eased away, saying, "What do you say we get out of here, Jim? I don't like your ponds right now."

I thought of how I'd saved this place for myself, so it couldn't get ruined. I said, "Sure, Jean. I'll get the canoe and pick up the ducks and we'll get moving."

"The canoe?" she said, smiling bravely. "You don't swim for them anymore?"

I couldn't quite smile back. "Not in the snow," I said. "I'm too old for that now." I said I'd be back in a second and I headed through the willows to the river.

We'd swum for a duck once in Wisconsin, the first fall after high school. I'd hit him and he'd set his wings and crashed far out in the lake. I said I'd get the canoe and Jean teased, "Oh just swim out there and get him, you big baby." For some reason I started peeling off my clothes. We got to laughing and before I knew what was happening Jean was out of her clothes too, and we were racing for that duck. It was a pretty, sunny day, but the water couldn't have been much over fifty degrees.

I reached the duck first and threw it back to her. For a second she put its neck in her mouth and started dog-paddling. But she started laughing so hard she threw the duck back to me and struck out for shore. She beat me back and when I got there she was prancing around naked, hugging herself. We were still laughing, but swearing too about the cold. Then Jean touched her nipples, rock hard and pointed with the cold. She laughed even harder and said, "Well, I guess the turkey is done."

I hadn't seen her like that in years, since she'd started her modeling drive, and I looked at her, feeling suddenly lost, and I stopped laughing. She said, "You know? Like those plastic things they put in the turkeys that pop up when they're done?"

I'd gotten her joke. That wasn't what I suddenly hadn't understood. I turned away from her and got into my clothes, before the sun had had a chance to dry me. Behind me I could hear Jean doing the same. She went to New York later that month and though I saw her after that, that was our last hunt together.

I'd forgotten all about it until she mentioned the swimming. Now it was as clear as yesterday. I couldn't get over how absolutely perfect she had been.

I went back to her with the canoe over my head, crashing through the willows and calling her name so she wouldn't think I was a moose. When I was out of the brush I swung the canoe down and saw Jean.

She was sitting on the bank, knees drawn tight to her chest, arms wrapped around her legs, shivering, naked as could be. Her hair clung to her head and wrapped around her neck, tracing the path of her spine, water still snaking down her back. Beside her the four ducks were stretched in a row.

"Oh, Jesus, Jean," I blurted, throwing my coat around her. She gave a weak smile, her lips blue. "What the hell are you trying to do?" I said, too loudly. "Are you trying to kill yourself? This isn't Wisconsin, Jean."

She just shrugged at me and her teeth chattered.

"Jesus, Jean. It's twenty degrees out."

"I didn't want to be too old anymore," she said.

As soon as I'd seen her I'd started tearing out handfuls of grass and I piled them together and broke down some of the dead willow. There were old beaver sticks along the banks too, and I piled those on. The grass went like lightning when I touched the match to it.

"Jesus, Jean," I said again. I helped her up and walked her to the fire. It burned wildly, dancing through the long dried wood, melting the snow in the sky. Jean just stood beside it and I turned her now and then until she stopped shivering. I looked to make sure she was dry and I got her long johns from the neat pile of clothing she'd left at the bank.

"Are you warm enough?" I asked.

"Yes," she said. "Thanks."

I held the union suit out but she was looking down at herself. "Look at these," she said, and I followed her point to the ragged quilt work of stretch marks along her sides and belly. I moved behind her and lifted a leg and slipped the cloth around it. I did the same with her other foot and pulled the underwear up her long body. I grabbed an arm and shoved it through the sleeve. She reached her other arm out, like a lady being helped with her coat. I slipped the sleeve over her hand.

I came around front again but she was buttoning the underwear herself, mechanically. "My children have made me hideous," she whispered.

"God you can talk some shit!" I swore. "You're the most perfect thing I've ever imagined."

186

She smiled then and looked at me. "You know, Jim," she said, "ever since I was a little girl I always thought it was such a shame we couldn't get married, you and I."

I smiled a little then too, surprised. "Me too," I said.

"Is that why you've waited?"

"Oh for Chrissakes. No. I haven't waited."

She stepped forward and hugged me so hard I could feel the bones of her. "I love you," she said, adding, "Bro'."

"Me too," I whispered. I made myself break out of the hug and I picked up her pants, my hands trembling as I held a leg for her to step through.

I could feel her looking at me, but she didn't say anything before she put her foot through the pants' leg. Then she whispered, "Jim, Jim, handsome and tall, who is the fairest of them all?" She laughed a little I think, some kind of sound like that. "God," she said, "how did you ever get away?"

"It was the last thing I wanted to do."

She let her hand rest on my shoulder and she said, "They mate for life, don't they? The geese?"

I said, "Yes, they do," and I thought of her in the snow, holding her shotgun at her side while all the geese flew so determinedly away from her.

"Do you remember, back in Wisconsin, when we'd sit in the blind and hope the geese would come into our duck decoys. Sometimes they'd come so close you'd whisper, 'Now if they'll just turn.' But they never once made that wrong turn, did they?"

"No. They're too smart."

"Even then I wished I was a goose," Jean said, and she took her hand away from me. "Remember the time I wouldn't let you shoot that one by himself?"

"You said he was too beautiful."

She laughed weakly. "At night I'd think how I was just like that goose. I knew I was that beautiful. And I thought I was that smart." She shook her head. "God, I was obnoxious. But I thought I had that. I thought all of that."

"I would've thought it for you if you hadn't."

"It was a long time before I realized I wasn't like that."

I picked at the nearly frozen dirt while Jean stood inches behind me. "Nobody's like that, Jean."

"I was."

"Well, welcome back," I said. "I'd rather have a sister than a goose anyway." I stood and held out her coat and she turned to let me help her.

I smoothed the coat over her shoulders and turned up the collar, lifting her wet hair over it. "We better be going, Jean," I said.

"I still wish I was a goose, Jim. Mated for life."

I ran her heavy hair through my fingers but couldn't say anything. I turned and picked up the canoe. She followed me but with the canoe scraping against the willows it was hard to hear when she spoke. I shouted, "What?"

She ducked under the canoe with me and said, "My kids. I didn't mean the way I looked. I didn't mean that's what they'd done to me."

I waited, then said, "What did you mean?" but she didn't answer. She said, "It sounds funny under here, doesn't it? Like everything is hollow."

"It's always like that."

"I would've liked to have heard that before," she said. "That empty sound. When it didn't mean anything except that I had a canoe over my head."

I told her to watch out and I swung the canoe down on the edge of the river. I pushed the boat into the current and held it. Jean picked her paddle from the bushes and stepped into the backseat, the guide's position. I started to say something but she just said, "Let me steer. I haven't done that in so long."

I said something about experience and how I better be the guide, but she said, "Can I stay here awhile, Jim? Can I stay with you?"

I could barely get the words out, but I said, "Of course." Then I sat down in the front seat, where I had no control, a place I hadn't been since high school, and Jean pushed the canoe into the current.

feller

I suppose the guys out in the woods get all the glamour, but that just shows how ignorant the general public can be. Trees there, softwoods, grow like toothpicks. Big toothpicks sure, that must be some dangerous, but nothing like these elms. And those guys can drop them anywhere, like pick-up-sticks. They'd be lost with power lines and light poles and fences and houses. I'd just like to see one of them take a look at one of these dead old elms, knowing he was going to have to drop it in the middle of this little quiet suburb street. I'd like to see his face when he got that knowledge.

When I first got this contract, a big one for just me and Troy, a huge one, Teri and I came up to Great Falls to get a motel and find where everything was. We drove down street after street, all canopied over with eighty-year-old elms, each one like a giant hand, reaching to grab a part of heaven. I like trees and I felt bad for them, knowing the disease had got them before they could close their fingers around whatever it was that'd made them grow so. But Teri just whistled soft, through her teeth like she'll do, and said, "Think you can do it?"

I was a little stunned myself, seeing them all for the first time, but I never wondered that. I didn't look at Teri. It wasn't like she was trying to get in a dig, but nowadays that wasn't automatic, that she wasn't trying to do that. "Hell," I said, "this'll go like clockwork."

We drove around a little more but it wasn't much fun after that and we went back to the motel and booked two rooms, a month at a time. Troy was coming over with the bucket truck and the way it ran there was no telling when he might get in.

We finally heard him next door around midnight, which meant he either had trouble with the carburetor or he'd stopped off someplace on the way, for a what he'd swear was just a game of pool.

Teri and I hadn't been talking much, just lying in bed with the TV down to no sound, the way she likes to leave it at night, and I knew she'd been listening for Troy as much as I had. Like he was our kid or something, late home on a school night. He wasn't more than a few years younger than me, but that's what it felt like in the dark of the room, with just the TV light.

Once we'd heard him knock around and flush and settle down we turned to each other in the new bed and settled in ourselves, christening that bed the way that'd been our habit ever since I started doing out-of-town jobs. But even then, even while we were at it, I was thinking of those trees, and how careful I'd have to be with them. Most of them had branches reaching more than halfway across the street, touching the branches of the ones on the other side.

When we were done Teri rolled over and I spooned in behind her, still holding her hand, our fingers tying in with each other's. We were always good at sleeping together.

We came from out east, Miles City, where I have a tree service. I'd dropped trees before, might even say a lot of them, but that next morning, early, with the frost white on the parkways, Troy and me stood in front of the first one we were going to take out. He was grinning a little, which, strange as it sounds, was a pretty good sign he'd stopped for a game last night and wasn't feeling so good.

The city was going to follow us around with a truck and a loader but nobody'd showed yet. I was supposed to get a final go-through of the ground rules by their parks guy, but I really wanted to get one down before anybody came to watch. Teri'd known that. She never sleeps in much, but she had this morning, saying she'd be along in a while. She was going to do cleanup, raking and stuff, so there really wasn't much need for her right off.

The whole time Troy was grinning I'd been eyeballing that big old tree, the sprayed-on yellow X crinkled deep over the old bark. I told Troy to pull the bucket truck up and I went to the tree and tore off the number tag that'd been stapled in at head height. It used to be red, but had faded to a kind of dull pink, and I put it in my pocket. I was trying to see which way this old tree wanted to come down.

I took a big breath and went up in the bucket with my little saw. I made the first balancing cuts, cutting the west-side branches so she'd drop just so. Some of the branches hung up where they'd grown in with their neighbor's across the street, and I had to move the bucket so I could pull them out. Leaving them there would just be making so many widow-makers for me and Troy.

When I finished trimming her I lowered myself to the ground and walked a circle around that first tree. I could tell she was going to come down pretty as a picture, no cabling or anything. I could see it all in my head, the shivering crack and the swoosh before the crash.

I took my big saw then and dove it in, making the wedge cut, the cut that gives the tree the idea what direction it wants to go. Troy was standing there behind me, holding on to the hammer and the plastic felling wedges, but I already knew we weren't going to need those.

I knocked the wedge loose and stepped back, eyeing my cut and knew I had it that right. I knew we were thinking alike, me and that tree, and I moved in to make the flat, felling cut. I started on one end of the wedge and wrapped it around, cutting deep, and I knew I had her.

The bark gave its little quiver and I glanced up, seeing the top start to tip. I stepped aside in case it kicked back, and I killed the saw and watched her go. Could've driven a spike with her, she fell so clean and straight.

Never even noticed the city guys there, already standing beside their truck, lightening their thermoses. One of them gave me a thumbs-up and I grinned, though the tree lay there all busted in the street.

Teri pulled up then too. She bailed out of our truck in her jeans and ratty work sweatshirt. Her hair, shiny and barely red, like polished heartwood, was already drawn back into her working ponytail. I watched the guys from the city watching her, and that made me smile too, right over the hulk of that tree. She's older than me, getting to be—what do they call it? thirty-something? I never used to think of her as older—she still turns heads, mine too sometimes, though things like that seem to be the first thing you stop noticing. Somehow it turns around that instead of staring at your wife, who really is a beautiful tomboy, you'll stare at other guys staring at her, like that means something. Twisted kind of, and I don't know why that is.

Teri met me and gave me a swat on the back, like football players do. "One down, a million to go," she said, laughing. While Troy climbed up onto the trunk and flexed his muscles like Popeye, I pushed my glasses up onto my forehead and brushed some wood chips off my face. The city guys came over and we all had a cup of coffee.

It reminded me of one of those old pictures of African safaris, with us laughing it up, having drinks and posing over the dead animal. I felt the way the guy with the gun always looked in the pictures, proud, you know, but a little scared, like the adrenaline is leaving and he doesn't know how he'll stand without that support. I lifted my coffee cup like a toast and put my arm around Teri's waist. She smiled then and I could feel the others' eyes on us, even without looking. But Teri discovered a reason to be someplace else pretty quick, and I took the few steps to the great fallen elm and stood over it alone. She never was much for touching, not when other people were around.

After they're down you might think the hard part's over and everything's just cruising from there. But think how those trees look standing up, arms reaching all over. That's still how they look lying down, like they can't give up trying to reach whatever it was they needed. You've got branches spread on the ground holding it up and you've got branches still way over your head, pointing sideways now, instead of straight up, but still outweighing you a hundred to one and still dangerous.

Cut the wrong branch out of the bottom and the whole thing loses the balance it's been growing its whole life. They'll turn on you then, rolling over quick to find some new balance, and if you're not quick yourself they'll crush you flat. That's how it gets if you ever start getting lazy, or even just start thinking they'll treat you like they did the day before, just because that's the way you'd like it. Hardly anything'll do that for you.

I studied that first downed tree, not really scared about what could happen, just trying to see how this one was. Trying to let myself see and know how it wanted to go. Seeing and knowing. Two different things. I blocked out Teri and the rest of them and picked up my saw.

When I took this job I planned on it taking at least a year to drop all the elms. That's why we started in the fall, instead of waiting for spring. And somehow I thought things might turn around if Teri and I got out of our apartment, moved around a little, saw something besides the same old streets and people in Miles City. That wasn't the smartest thing I ever came up with. I doubt living out of a motel room for twelve months ever made anything anywhere any better. I'd tried to make it sound like a vacation, but she's not an idiot.

Even when the cold snaps hit I didn't chance a layoff. I didn't think right then that me and Teri'd last through a layoff. I worked us straight through the coldest of everything. Nobody expected that, not the city or Troy or Teri, but the city sure didn't mind, the quicker the better. And Troy—only other thing he'd've done was gone back to Miles City and collected unemployment. Working in the cold was a bitch, but it beat watching game shows and soap operas all day. Teri took it right in stride, like she does everything.

Felling was no cakewalk, bundled up as we'd get. During the worst of it we'd be the only people out on the streets, and moving so stiff and awkward with the clothes and the cold we began to feel like moon walkers. That's what Teri called us each morning, when we'd leave with our thermoses still steaming around the necks from what we'd spilled. And she started calling Great Falls the dark side of the moon. She wasn't working with us anymore—couldn't rake anything up in the snow. I wasn't sure what she did all day, but I should've seen it'd be worse than any kind of layoff we could've done together.

At work Troy and I'd gotten into this game where he'd take the wedge piece I'd cut and set it in the middle of the street. I'd have to hit it with the tree when I dropped it. And not just nick it either, but nail it, so it couldn't be pulled out until we cut up the tree.

I missed a few early on. Grazed one once that launched out spinning, a good six feet off the ground. Went twenty-seven feet on the fly. Troy stepped it off. I'd heard it whistling even as the tree was grinding into the street, like some giant chunk of shrapnel, and I couldn't shake that sound all the rest of the day. It was a jagged, moaning whistle, something dangerous, all because I'd been so close, but not dead-on. Should've quit screwing with it then, but it got to mean something, and I didn't miss another after that. Then it got to be a streak thing, where hitting that wedge with a whole tree seemed like the most important thing I did all day.

We had a thaw in late February, that started to mush up the snow and sink it down before it froze again. After that the snow was like pavement. It was hard to trust at first, and we'd walk around on tiptoes, expecting to crash through the crust every step. But pretty soon, just like anything, we got to thinking that's how it always was, and we didn't think about it again until it got warm and we started breaking through. Teri started working again and it was something to see her raking away, sifting in piles of broken sticks and branches, all on top of a field of snow. Made me a little dizzy sometimes, like she was walking on air, or on something like that, where she wasn't supposed to be.

I was surprised to see how excited she got about the wedge game. At first I was embarrassed to even show her. It was pretty juvenile when you thought about it. But I'd smacked more than three hundred in a row and Troy wasn't going to let me stop. I was glad of that, especially when I saw Teri didn't laugh at it. It really was all I looked forward to. I was awful good at it. When I'd drill one Troy'd whoop but Teri'd just stick her fist straight up in the air, the old power sign. You wouldn't believe how I'd live just to see that.

Nights I was at a loose end, usually just sitting in the motel room watching Teri. When she'd first started showing up in the bars after her divorce, a little older than we were used to and not all that anxious to have anything to do with us, she just drove me wild. I cut the brim off my baseball cap one day, bucking up brush and thinking about what she'd be like, not paying attention at all when a tooth caught something wrong and kicked the whole saw back. That close to cutting off my face.

Now I was sitting in a motel room watching her buck-ass naked on the bed, bored, flipping through the TV channels, and all I could think about was the trees I was going to fell in the morning. Sometimes I'd go out at night and study them, figuring where their balance was, thinking how the wedge cut would let us each know where she wanted to come down. Most times Teri'd be asleep when I'd come back, with the heat on too high, and the TV light gloomy and the silence of it everywhere in the little room. I'd never gotten used to that habit of hers. TVs aren't supposed to be silent, and it made me almost scared. Like the silence grew out of the room, or even out of her, making the room hot and uncomfortable all by itself.

I'd stand there then, watching Teri in the blue light. She'd be naked still, too hot even for a sheet, and I'd go over every inch of her. I sometimes thought how she looked even better with clothes on, when I still had to use my imagination.

I'd turn off the heat then and open a window and climb into bed. I'd pull the blankets up over us and she'd come right into me, because I was still cold from outside and she was too warm. Then we'd heat up and she'd move away. Then the open window would do its trick and the whole room would get cold and she'd move back in, till we touched everywhere at once, for warmth. I don't know if she even woke up during any of her moves. Like I said, we were always good at sleeping together.

In the spring, with all the snow gone, we really started to pick up speed again. We were all going a little crazy stuck in the motel and I started pushing it. We'd always gone dawn to dusk, just because there was nothing else to do, but I started humping a little harder when we were out, so we'd be worn out by the time we got home and lying around doing nothing wouldn't seem like such a bad thing.

Teri started going out some nights with Troy, but I never did that. I couldn't work with a hangover the way Troy could. I couldn't get the feel of the trees—couldn't see the balance. So I'd stay in the room till I couldn't stand it, then go out and look at the next day's trees. Got to where I'd have the trees figured out two days in advance, even three. Most times Teri'd be in by the time I got back, other times she'd come in afterward.

The nights she'd come in late she'd be shivering when she jumped into the bed and she'd giggle about the temperature. "Jesus Christ," she'd say. "Colder than a grave in here. What are you, some kind of reptile? Some kind of cold-blooded critter?" She'd be crunching into me then, feeling around with her hands, her skin covered with goose bumps that'd go away and that I'd try to bring back. Her hair'd smell like cigarette smoke and when we kissed, or even when her breath was just near my face, I could smell the beer or whiskey. Then she'd laugh again and holding on to me she'd say, "Oh, no. Not cold-blooded at all. Not one bit."

Sometimes she'd be out long enough she'd forget to turn on the TV when she came in. Then, wrestling around in the cold, dark room, things could get as exciting as they'd been at first. Once she didn't come back till bar time and at first I was too tired, but she was really wound-up and pretty soon she got me that way too and we really got after it. Troy started beating on the wall, and I could hear him laughing and shouting, "What the hell you two doing in there? Killing each other?"

Teri about died with that one. She was on top of me and she just stopped and started to laugh until I thought she might never be able to take another breath. Finally she had to roll off me and tuck herself into a ball, arms around her ribs, like that'd save her from suffocating.

I didn't think it was all that funny. Teri was my wife, for crying out loud, and we were trying to make something together, and it didn't seem like it was working, no matter how much noise we could make at night. Tell the truth, what I wanted to do was go over and beat the shit out of Troy. I'd never felt that way before, but with Teri rolled up with her back to me, the giggles finally dying, I felt like I'd explode if I didn't smack something.

Instead, I rolled over to face Teri's back and I traced the wiry ridge of muscle on each side of her backbone. Sure enough goose bumps sprang up right behind my fingers. Somehow she knew how funny I thought it was, and she finally whispered, like she was more exhausted than she'd ever been in her life, "Can't you see it, Jack? Can't you fucking see it?"

"I guess not," I said.

"That's exactly what we're doing. That drunk little punk knows more about it than we do."

"What do you mean?" I didn't feel like smacking anything then. I felt like curling up into my own ball. But for an instant I wondered about Troy. I wondered what he'd look like if he took the place of one of those wedges I hit with every tree.

"We're killing each other, just like he said." She inched backward until we were spoons in the bed. I put my arm around her and she covered it with hers. We were experts.

"Why do you think I leave the TV on all the time?"

"I don't know."

"Because I'm afraid of the dark."

When I didn't say anything she said, "And I leave the heater on because I'm afraid to be cold."

I still didn't say anything. She said, "You didn't know that, did you?"

"I guess not."

"How could you?" she said. "I leave the sound off so we can talk, but we never do."

"We talk sometimes."

"Never," she said. "Sometimes I think the silence and the dark are the same thing. I get them mixed up sometimes.

"And you," she hugged my arm tighter, "you walk around by yourself in the dark, planning how to kill trees."

"That's not what I'm planning."

"Oh, I know. You love them right enough. I can see that. But you kill them every day."

"They're already dead."

"But they're still standing! You won't even leave them that much."

"Teri," I said, holding her as tight as I could, like I could squeeze out poison. "They're trees, dead ones. This isn't about trees."

"You don't get it at all, do you?"

"Get what?"

"What do you look at at night?" she asked. "What the hell do you think about?"

I thought of watching her stretched naked in the shifting blue light, with nothing left to the imagination. I said, "I think about balance."

"Balance?"

"Don't you ever see them? They look like hands. Like they spent their whole lives reaching for something."

"Like what?"

"I don't know."

"They never get there, do they?"

"No."

"What do you suppose they're after?"

"I don't know."

"Do you have any idea how many times you say that? Makes me want to scream."

"Well, I *don't* know!" I said, my voice getting too loud. "I keep wondering what we can do to make it work, but I don't know what it is."

"I don't know if we can do anything."

I kept on holding her and I tried to imagine what it'd be like without her. We'd only been married a couple years and imagining that was easier than I would've guessed. It made me afraid of myself.

"It's light they're after," Teri whispered all of a sudden. "Plain and simple."

When I still didn't say anything, she said, "A divorce wouldn't kill me. I've lived through it before. Though I was damn sure I'd never do it again."

I really didn't want a divorce but I couldn't think of anything to say. There was no balance here.

She didn't say anything else for a long, long time, and it was almost peaceful there in the darkness. I was hoping she'd fallen asleep. Then she finally whispered, "I'll leave in the morning. As soon as it gets light. I just can't do one more thing in the dark."

I still couldn't think of anything to say. I said, "I don't want you to go."

"Oh, I know that. But I've got to get out of the dark. I can't stand it anymore."

"Maybe you'll come back," I said.

"Yeah," she said, and I was surprised to feel she was crying. "Maybe I will."

The next morning Troy and I went out with the first of the light and we started with a tree that had a natural lean to it. Not even any bucket work. I'd looked her over two nights before and I knew which way she wanted to fall and I dug the saw in, making the wedge cut, knowing we were thinking alike.

Troy took the wedge out and set it in the street, glancing up just a second to position it. He was grinning hard and I knew he was in quite a bit of pain. He hadn't mentioned Teri not coming out with us.

I looked at the wedge and then at the tree and I bent down for the felling cut. Started on one end of the wedge and wrapped it around, cutting deep, and I knew I had her. When I saw her shiver I stepped back and killed the saw.

She toppled like all the rest, slow at first, as if she still thought there was something she could do to stop it, but then going fast, like she had to get it over with quick as she could. Drilled the wedge dead center.

Troy didn't even bother whooping, just grinned and nodded his head a little. I looked toward the next tree, trying to remember which one it was and how it was balanced.

There at the end of the street was our pickup. Teri was at the wheel, hanging halfway out the window. She'd been watching me drop that elm and she was looking right at my eyes. But she dropped her head when I saw her and she stuck her fist straight up into the sky. The same old power sign as ever.

Without looking back up she slipped inside the cab and started away. Standing behind me Troy said, "I sure hope she got the number of the truck that hit me last night."

I looked over at him, where he was rubbing sheepishly at his head and I remembered I'd wanted to drop a tree on him, for something that was my fault and no one else's. He smiled and said, "I hope she's going for coffee."

I pulled the faded red tag off the next dead elm and my hand shook a little as I put it in my pocket with the others. The bottom of the pocket was soft with old wood chips and I thumbed the frayed edge of the tag, feeling how worn it was. I said, "I hope she is too."

the topic
OF CANCER

L eaning close, nearly touching Duncan's face, Mickey couldn't stop himself from looking for a glimpse of Carol. But the warmth of his son's breath touched Mickey's cheek and, closing his eyes, Mickey released the seat belt and eased Duncan from the truck without waking him.

Cradling Duncan's head against his shoulder, Mickey turned to the rented beach house, wondering if there was another child in America who would volunteer to skip the plane ride, who would say he'd rather drive even after Mickey sat him down with a map, showing the distance from Laramie, Wyoming, to Ocean Beach, New Jersey.

"From our home to our vacation," Duncan had called it.

At the time Mickey worried that the distance and time were incomprehensible to a six-year-old, but through the four hard days on the road Duncan had sat for hours staring out the window at everything they passed, even when it seemed for hours they passed nothing. He slept sitting up, napping like he hadn't in years. It was

Mickey who pestered Duncan about stopping to eat, about stopping to pee, not the other way around.

When Duncan talked it had been in long spurts: about his friends, about seeing the ocean. Late the first day he asked, "Did Mom ever see a ocean?"

Mickey had stammered, "No," then, "she was from Wyoming." When Duncan kept looking at him, kept waiting, Mickey'd pointed at whatever they were passing, asking, "Have you ever seen anything like that, Dunc'?" It was something ridiculous, a fence or something, and Duncan hadn't bothered answering. And he hadn't brought up Carol again for a long time.

But at the end of every day, when they pulled into the night's motel, Duncan made Mickey promise that they weren't moving to New Jersey, even though it's where all his uncles and aunts lived, his grandparents and cousins. He made Mickey promise that as soon as the vacation was over they'd go back home to Wyoming, where they'd always lived. Mickey wondered if Duncan'd listened in on Mickey's parents' calls after Carol's funeral: "There's no reason anymore, Mickey, for you to be so far away."

Now, in the predawn gloom, Mickey carried Duncan down the skinny walkway between the tightly packed vacation homes. When he'd called yesterday, his parents had told him how excited the whole family was to see the two of them; that they'd leave the door unlocked if he really thought they had to come in the middle of the night.

It was closer to dawn than the middle of the night, but they'd made the last haul through the night, Mickey wanting Duncan back on schedule for his family. He didn't want any scenes now, everyone else already together long enough to discuss his situation, ready to look for signs anywhere, even in Duncan, to betray the hardships.

The rust-hinged screen screeched, and Mickey stretched Duncan out on the narrow bed. Taking a step back, he sat on the made-up cot. He watched Duncan sleep, openmouthed the way Carol had. He lowered his face to his hands, rubbing his stubbled cheeks, exhausted beyond sleep.

But he tried, swinging his legs up on the cot, feeling in the first moment how the center bar would cut into his back. The cot, he knew, was meant for Duncan, and tonight Duncan would fight him for the novelty of it. Fight and win, Mickey thought. He lifted his arm over his eyes, glancing at his watch. Quarter to five in the morning.

Within a minute the skin of Mickey's arm and forehead was slicked with sweat. The air was heavy and briny, something he'd almost forgotten in the high dry of Carol's Wyoming. Mickey sat up, blowing out a long, quiet breath.

Scattering T-shirts and underwear across the cot until he found his swim trunks, Mickey slipped out of his shoes and jeans. He stood to slip on the trunks, but caught his foot and crash-landed back on the cot. He sat there naked, his foot caught in the neon blue nylon, and saw Duncan watching him, three feet away.

"Go back to sleep," Mickey whispered, tugging at the trunks. "Excitement's over. Nothing to see here."

"Are you going swimming?"

"Just hot," Mickey lied, glancing at his watch again. Duncan had been sleeping since Pittsburgh. Seven hours. Though Mickey'd thought of actually being alone, of walking into the water with no one to watch, even of the beautiful fuss his parents would make over finding their grandson when they woke, he couldn't help asking, "Want to?"

Duncan shot up, wriggling out of his jeans. He was already wearing his trunks, like underwear.

Mickey blinked. "When did you put those on?"

"At the motel. I never swam in a ocean before. I never even seen a ocean."

Pulling two towels from the folded stack, Mickey said, "We'll still be back before anybody gets up."

Duncan took hold of two of Mickey's fingers, a habit he'd revived in the year since the funeral, and they walked the twisting little streets together, Duncan dropping his hand often enough to pick up a stick or broken bits of seashells. He threw the stick into a dead-end waterway identical to the one bordering their cabin, bristling with pleasure boats. "What's the ocean going to be like?" he asked.

"Big."

"How big?"

"Huge."

"How huge?"

Mickey blew out a breath, swinging through a circle, looking for landmarks in the flat crowd of mechanically quaint houses. Lost now without mountains.

"How huge?" Duncan asked again.

"You'll see it in a second, Dunc'," Mickey answered, bending down and waving him over. Duncan ran holding out his arms and Mickey swung him onto his shoulders.

With Duncan's legs clamped around his ears, Mickey walked almost an entire block before Duncan's next question. "Dad?" he asked.

Mickey sighed. "What Dunc'?"

"What's the Topic of Cancer?"

Mickey glanced at his hands, tight around Duncan's ankles. "What?"

"The Topic of Cancer. What is it?"

"Tropic," Mickey whispered. "I think you mean, Tropic. It's geography."

"But it's in the ocean, isn't it?"

"It's only a line somewhere," Mickey answered. "Like longitude. It's nothing real."

"Oh," Duncan said. "I thought maybe Mom went there."

Mickey looked out at the ocean, visible now between the last row of houses, a fog hiding the flat line of the horizon. "No," Mickey said, the word sticking in his throat. "I told you about Mom. It's not that kind of cancer. It doesn't . . ."

"Oh," Duncan said, stopping him.

He carried Duncan down the path between the last of the beach houses, wondering what else he could say. But as soon as he stepped onto the sand Duncan kicked his heels against his chest, squirming until Mickey could put him down. He ran toward the water, shouting, "Think it'll be warm?"

"I don't know," Mickey answered, stepping more quickly, the sand clutching at his feet. "Slow up," he called. "Wait for me till you go in."

But the flat sand, hard and wet beyond the reach of waves, was something different, and suddenly Duncan stepped more slowly. Mickey fell in beside him. The water itself was still and slick, barely lapping the edge of the beach. The red ball of the sun burned and wavered through the mist.

"I thought there'd be waves," Duncan said.

"There'll be some before we leave. You'll get to surf."

"I don't know how."

Mickey looked down at him, his bare feet making little prints in the damp sand. "I'll teach you, Dunc'," he said.

Duncan asked, "How did it get wet all the way up here if there's no waves?"

"The tide must be going out."

"What's the tide?"

Mickey rubbed his forehead. "Something the moon does. The ocean moves up and down. Every day."

Duncan glanced over his shoulder. "The moon?" he said, smiling.

Mickey reached for him, but he jumped away, ripping down the tidemark, the sand as hard as a street.

Mickey let him run, thinking of the hours and hours trapped in the car, but then gave chase, closing in tight. Duncan shivered and giggled as Mickey touched his naked back, so close to really catching him.

Then Mickey dashed to the side, careening into the ocean. The water was much warmer than he'd guessed, nearly bathtub warm, and the sand did not deepen its pitch, but stretched out endlessly, leaving Mickey running through ankle-deep water, then knee-deep, when he'd thought he'd be able to splash in and dive under before Duncan could react.

He heard Duncan splashing in behind him and Mickey was so proud of his chasing him right into something so unknown he had to fight the tears he'd kept back ever since realizing how badly they frightened his son.

"You can't get me!" Mickey shouted, but he was slowing and slowing, waiting for the touch.

And when he felt the small hands, the nails that needed trimming, Mickey turned, catching Duncan and falling. Duncan followed him under, grabbing at his neck, his head. Even under water Mickey thought he could hear him laughing.

Mickey kicked away from the bottom, the sand out here as hard as it was onshore, and threw himself into the air, still holding Duncan tight. But he only shouted, "I got you!" pounding his fists against Mickey's shoulders.

Then, abruptly, Duncan stopped. "Yuck," he said, licking his lips.

"Salt," Mickey explained. He flipped Duncan onto his back, letting him loose. "Float," he said, and Duncan did, his eyes going wide at the new corklike properties of his body.

He struggled up, the water making a line beneath his narrow chest. He gave Mickey his can-you-believe-what-we've-discovered stare, and said, "Let's go deeper."

And though they played the whole way out, when Duncan's toes suddenly lost their hold on the bottom, the water floating him free, he asked about sharks, turning back for shore before Mickey could answer. Mickey had to follow him in, saying there weren't any sharks here, there wouldn't be a beach if there were, they wouldn't allow swimming, it was perfectly safe.

"Nothing's perfectly safe," Duncan answered, trudging toward the empty beach.

Mickey stopped, then started after him again. "Come on," he said. "We can play here. Even if there were sharks, they couldn't swim in this far. It's too shallow."

"Sharks can swim in six inches of water."

"How do you know?" Mickey asked. Then, "There's no sharks, Duncan."

Duncan wavered, but kept going. He put his arms around himself. "I'm cold then," he said.

So they walked the beach, Duncan finding shell after shell, asking for identifications Mickey couldn't give. "How come the water's salty?" he asked.

"All oceans are salty."

"How come?"

"Because they're the oceans. They're salt water."

"How come?"

Mickey looked back to where they'd entered the beach, making sure he could remember the house. "Evapomasstranspiration," he mumbled.

"Oh," Duncan answered, picking up the husk of a horseshoe crab. He sat down with it, scraping at the sand with the shovel-like shell. Mickey sat beside him.

Duncan dug his shell deep into the beach, quietly heaping up sloppy stacks of wet sand. "Dad?" he asked.

Mickey couldn't help rolling his eyes. "What, Dunc'?"

"Do you even miss Mom?"

Mickey's mouth worked a second without making a sound. "What? Of course I do."

"Oh," Duncan said. He waited before asking, "Then how come you don't talk about her?"

Mickey reached out to smooth Duncan's wild hair, but it was dry already, salt-hardened spikes added to the tangle. Searching for something to say he glanced at the sun, still a red ball, still something possible to look at, and suddenly the word *ovary* sprang into his head, and Mickey wondered if that's what Carol's had looked like, that overwhelming. "Dunc'?" he said, just to keep from gasping.

"Huh?"

"You mind if I take a swim?" He took a breath. "You could build a big huge sand castle. When I get back we can bomb it."

Duncan kept working, digging the moat. "I don't want to bomb it," he said.

"Okay. We can just keep building it, bigger and bigger. The biggest ever." Mickey looked away from the sun.

"Okay."

"You'll stay right here? Like we've talked about? You won't talk to anyone?"

Duncan glanced one way down the deserted beach, then the other.

"People will start coming. It's getting late."

Mickey stood up, stepping toward the water, looking away from the ball of the sun. "Really. Stay right here."

Duncan nodded, still digging.

"Dunc'?"

"Okay, Dad!" he said sharply, still not lifting his head.

Mickey watched him a moment more. "I'll be right back. You can watch me."

"Okay."

When Mickey stepped into the water, Duncan finally looked up. "Watch out for sharks," he said.

Mickey walked farther out. He turned, raising his voice. "I can swim faster than any old shark," he said, wishing it was true. Any old cancer. "You know that."

"Nobody can do that."

"I can," Mickey yelled. "I'm your dad."

Duncan still watched him, doubting, and Mickey dove.

He swam beneath the surface as long as he could, biting his lips shut, the word *ovary* blinding. For Christ's sake, the Topic of Cancer. He swam hard, kicking against the water, lungs straining.

Not even bending over the hugeness of Carol's belly, talking to their child before they'd known he'd be a Duncan, not a Laura, were ovaries something they'd thought about. Not until the checkup, put off so long for so many perfectly good reasons, not until the biopsy came back with its sentence, did *ovary* become this word that could turn even the sun against him.

Mickey broke the surface at last, sucking in a huge breath. He heard a trace of Duncan calling, "Dad!" and he spun around, trying to stand but finding he'd swum past the bottom. He went under for a second, then kicked high, seeing Duncan standing by his castle, waving at him. The ocean had picked up; long, slow swells easing toward shore, and Duncan disappeared as Mickey sank into a hollow.

He'd stayed under too long, Mickey realized. He'd scared Duncan. He swam onto the next swell and kicked up, waving again, shouting, "I'm okay. No sharks."

Duncan waved back and then disappeared behind the swell running out from under Mickey.

Mickey turned, swimming out again. He stroked carefully, remembering how Carol had moved in the water, like something born there, an otter or something. But she'd never seen an ocean herself, and now he was swimming in one alone, her boy making sand castles behind him.

Though he'd meant to parallel the beach so Duncan could watch, Mickey kept swimming straight away from shore. Without Duncan back there on the beach, he thought, he might keep swimming. All the way to Carol. Clear to the Topic of Cancer.

Mickey swam a long time before finally rolling onto his back, his eyes closed against the sun's red ball. He bobbed in the salt the same way Duncan had earlier, with something of the same wonder. Sometimes he cried only because he was so glad there was still Duncan keeping him tethered to shore.

He bobbed there longer than he knew, wishing they could finish this visit and then drive somewhere else, the West Coast maybe, see another ocean. Then go on to the next, somewhere new, somewhere salty, the Gulf maybe, never slowing enough to let anything catch up.

With the sun red-black against his closed eyes, Mickey nearly dozed, only a rolling swell lifting his ears above the water to let him hear his name, again shouted across the sea. "Mickey!" this time, not "Dad!"

He turned slowly, wondering if he'd really heard such a thing, and when he kicked up to look he saw a crowd on the beach where he'd left Duncan and his stomach came into his mouth and he started swimming faster than he ever had in his life. Faster even than with Carol.

Though he could hardly breathe he turned his head anyway, exhaling by screaming his son's name into the salty water he flashed through. With every lifting swell, he pitched his head back, still swimming but searching the shore, the little group huddled at the water's edge waiting for him. The salt stung his eyes and the group remained nothing more than a horrifying blur, and he cast his head back into position, his arms and lungs burning. Swimming for Duncan. For Carol.

The group grew rapidly, Mickey wondering if he'd last long enough to reach them. But the next time he looked a tiny person broke free and dashed into the ocean, splashing toward him.

Mickey kept swimming, his head up, the rescue stroke he'd learned half his life ago. "Duncan!" he screamed, using breath he couldn't spare. He kept his head up long enough to hear "Dad!" then Mickey dropped his face back into the water, driving for the finish, and when he looked again Duncan was only yards away and Mickey scooped him up, throwing him clear of the ocean and catching him before he could touch down.

"What happened? What?" Mickey gasped, staggering in the last of the swells, the water streaming from his eyes until he could see that the group there, the people Duncan had broken away from, was his family, all of them, standing on the sand at the edge of the water, some only in robes, all staring at him.

Mickey pried Duncan a few inches from his chest, looked at his face, struggled for breath. "What?" he asked.

"The sharks!" Duncan answered sobbing, pushing his face back into Mickey's chest.

Mickey hugged him there, tottering toward shore, toward his family, shaking his head, asking with his eyes.

His mother stepped forward, shaking her own head, saying, "Mickey?" and nothing else, not *What in the world?*, not, *How could you?*, nothing but, "Mickey?" Then, "He was scared half to death."

Mickey hugged Duncan tighter, thinking what a sweet thing that would be; being scared only half to death.

"What happened?" Mickey asked again, reaching the sand, holding Duncan across his chest as he had when he was a baby.

His family opened for them, a half-moon pinning Mickey to the ocean's edge.

"He came bolting in like there was a fire," Mickey's father answered. "Everybody still in bed, him screaming, 'Sharks! Sharks! Sharks got Dad!'"

Mickey opened his mouth, but no words came. He glanced at his son, saw his eyes clamped tight, his cheeks burning red. He pictured the maze of streets, the identically cute cottages or bungalows or cabins, whatever they were called. He lifted Duncan as close to his face as he could.

"How in the world did you find them?" he asked.

Duncan bit his lip, twisting his face even farther to hide against his chest. "I remembered," he said, his voice stuttering over a sob.

"It's okay," Mickey whispered. "It's okay, Dunc'."

Mickey took a step forward, saying, "I'm sorry," then saying it again. "Everybody, I'm sorry. It's just . . ." He stopped, swinging Duncan up to his shoulder, the way he used to burp him after the bottle. It's just what? he wondered.

"Okay," Mickey's father said, herding his clan away from the swelling ocean. "Excitement's over. Nothing to see here."

Mickey tilted his head against Duncan's, murmuring to himself, "You are the best baby in the world. And you've got the best Mommy ever. You are going to be . . ." The old burping mantra.

Duncan clung to him, shaking his head against his shoulder. "I don't want to live here, Dad. I can't remember Mom here."

"I promised, Dunc'. Remember?"

"There's sharks here, Dad."

Mickey took a breath. "Your mom always wanted to see a shark. Did you know that?"

Duncan shook his head, turning just enough to look at him.

Mickey walked across the sand with his family. "She did," he whispered to his son. "She used to say I swam like a shark. Back when we first met."

"On the swim team?" Duncan asked.

Mickey nodded. "On the swim team," he repeated. "Before you were even a tadpole." That was Carol's line, but Duncan only leaned against him, waiting to hear more.

5.11.98   24.98   5T

Becker